THE SADDLE CLUB

BROKEN HORSE

BONNIE BRYANT

A SKYLARK BOOK
NEW YORK · TORONTO · LONDON · SYDNEY · AUCKLAND

RL 5, 009–012

BROKEN HORSE

A Bantam Skylark Book / December 1996

ISBN 0-553-48375-7

Published simultaneously in the United States and Canada.

PRINTED IN THE UNITED STATES OF AMERICA

OPM   0 9 8 7 6 5 4 3 2 1

*I would like to express my special thanks
to Catherine Hapka for her help
in the writing of this book.*

"I STILL THINK this would be a lot more fun on horseback," Carole Hanson joked breathlessly. It was a brisk Saturday afternoon in early December, and Carole and her two best friends, Lisa Atwood and Stevie Lake, were hiking in the state park just outside their hometown, Willow Creek, Virginia.

"You think everything would be more fun on horseback," Lisa joked back. That was true. But it was also true that Lisa and Stevie felt exactly the same way. The three girls loved horses and riding so much that they had formed The Saddle Club. Their club had only two rules: Members had to be horse-crazy, and they had to be willing to help each other out.

"Hold on a second. I've got another pebble," Stevie said.

She sat down on a large boulder and removed one of her shoes.

"We told you not to wear sneakers," Carole said, leaning against a tree trunk to rest. "What happened to the new hiking boots your grandparents gave you for your birthday?"

Stevie shrugged. "They're in my room somewhere. I think."

Carole and Lisa laughed. Stevie's room was famously messy, and it didn't surprise them that their friend had lost her hiking boots in the clutter.

While she waited for Stevie to extract the pebble from her shoe, Lisa pointed her camera at an interesting-looking tree. She fiddled with the lens, trying to get the top branches in focus. It was a clear, bright winter day, and she had been taking lots of pictures of the scenery.

"Are you getting some good shots for your project?" Carole asked.

"Definitely," Lisa said. She was doing a school science project on ecosystems, and she wanted to include plenty of photographs along with her written report. That was why she had suggested this hike. "It's amazing how much life there is out here in the woods even in the wintertime. These pictures will be a great way to show the relationships among all the different plants and animals we've seen today. And they'll make my report a lot more interesting."

Stevie finished lacing her sneaker and stood up. "Speaking of relationships," she said, "did I tell you the latest on the couple of the century?"

"I take it you mean Alex and his girlfriend?" Lisa asked as the girls continued along the wooded trail.

"Who else?" Stevie said. A few weeks ago her twin brother, Alex, had started dating a girl from school named Paige Dempsey. Stevie and her older brother, Chad, and younger brother, Michael, had been teasing Alex nonstop ever since.

"All your teasing isn't starting to come between them, is it?" asked Carole.

"Hardly," Stevie replied. "They don't even notice when I tease them most of the time. That's what I was going to tell you. I squirted some of Mom's good perfume onto Alex's favorite sweater so that Paige would think he'd been hanging out with another woman. But all she did was start batting her eyelashes and telling him how wonderful he smelled." She made a face. "They're absolutely sickening. How can they stand themselves?"

Lisa paused to take a picture of a small brown bird hopping busily among the dead leaves at the base of a bare-limbed oak tree. "Remember, this is Alex's first real romance. He's bound to be a little annoying about it."

Stevie snorted. "A *little* annoying? We'll see if you're still talking that way after you spend some time with him tonight. If he can tear himself away from the wonderful Paige long enough to come home, that is." The girls were having a sleepover at Stevie's house that night.

"Personally, I can't wait to get a look at the love-struck Alex," Carole said with a giggle. "I'm having trouble picturing it."

"Believe me, it sounds a lot more interesting than it actually is," Stevie said.

Lisa smiled. "Well, I think it's kind of cute that Alex has a girlfriend. Despite what you may think, Stevie, he's a nice guy. He deserves a little romance in his life."

"Gross. I'm just glad I'm not going to the school dance on Friday," Stevie declared, kicking a large dead branch off the trail so no one would trip on it. "I don't think my stomach could take it."

"I'm sure the last thing you'll be thinking about on Friday is Alex's love life," Carole said. Stevie's parents were taking the three girls into nearby Washington, D.C., to see a performance of the ballet *The Nutcracker*. That meant Stevie would be missing the annual holiday dance at Fenton Hall, the private school she and her brothers attended. Carole and Lisa went to the public school on the other side of Willow Creek.

"That's for sure," Lisa agreed. "I can't wait. *The Nutcracker* is my favorite ballet." Lisa knew a lot about ballet because she had been taking ballet lessons for years.

"It's the only ballet I've ever seen," Stevie admitted. "But I love it, too. It really puts me in the Christmas spirit."

"This will be my first time seeing it, but I think I know what you mean," Carole said. "There are certain things that make it seem like the holidays, aren't there? Like baking Christmas cookies and decorating the tree." Stevie and Lisa noticed that Carole's voice sounded wistful. Mrs. Hanson had died a few years ago. Even though Carole and her father were closer than ever, they both still missed her a lot, and their holidays were always a little bit sad.

Stevie knew one topic that would distract Carole. "I can't believe you forgot the most Christmassy thing of all," she said. "The Starlight Ride."

Pine Hollow, the stable where The Saddle Club rode, had lots of traditions, but the Starlight Ride was one of their favorites. Every Christmas Eve at seven P.M., all the young riders gathered at the stable for a lantern-lit ride through the wooded trails near Pine Hollow. The ride ended in the center of Willow Creek, where the whole town gathered to sing holiday songs and celebrate the season with the Starlight Riders. It was an unforgettable experience that The Saddle Club always looked forward to.

Carole smiled. "I didn't forget," she assured her friend. "I was just saving the best for last."

Stevie noticed that Lisa was taking another picture. "I can't believe you can even think about schoolwork when we're talking about the Starlight Ride."

"I'm listening," Lisa said. "I can't wait for Christmas, either. But first I have to finish my report. Can you believe how different the forest is now from the way it is in the summer?"

Stevie looked around and shrugged. "Sure," she said. "In the summer everything is green. Now everything's all brown and dead."

"But not totally," Lisa said. "It's amazing how much life there is if you look for it. It's just moved below the surface, that's all." She leaned over to focus on a beetle scurrying across a patch of earth.

Carole was still thinking about the Starlight Ride. "It seems like it's ages away, doesn't it?"

"It sure does," Stevie replied. She didn't even need to ask what Carole was referring to, because she had just been thinking the same thing.

Lisa looked up from her viewfinder. "Are you still talking about the Starlight Ride? It's less than three weeks away."

"I know," Carole said. "But that sounds like a long time to me."

"Me too," Stevie agreed.

"Me three," Lisa admitted. "But I'm sure it will seem closer when Christmas vacation starts the week after next." Fenton Hall and the Willow Creek public school system started their winter vacations at the same time.

The girls continued along the winding trail, which was becoming steeper as it climbed a heavily wooded hill. The air was chilly, and a light breeze made it seem even cooler, but the girls had been hiking for more than an hour and were warm with exertion. Lisa had kept them moving at a brisk pace as she hurried from one photo to the next.

Halfway to the top of the hill, Carole stepped off the trail and collapsed onto a smooth rock. "I don't know about you two, but I need a rest after all that climbing," she said, puffing.

"Good idea," Stevie said, sitting down beside her. "I think we're right at the edge of the park, anyway. We should probably head back soon."

Lisa was looking ahead at the craggy crest of the hill. "I'd like to take a look from the top there," she said. "There might be a good view of a valley or something on the other side. I only have a few pictures left on the roll, and most of my shots so far have been close-ups. It would be nice to get a photo of the whole landscape."

"Are you sure that's a good idea?" Carole asked. "If Stevie's right, you might be trespassing on private property." One of the things the owner of Pine Hollow, Max Regnery, had taught all his young riders was respect for others' land. One of his strictest rules was that no one could ride on private property without permission.

But Lisa didn't think this qualified. "Don't worry," she said. "I'm sure no one will mind if I just take a few pictures. You guys can wait here if you want. I'll be right back."

Carole and Stevie watched as their friend began scrambling up the last few dozen yards of steep trail.

"Can you believe how responsible she is?" Stevie commented. "All I can think about is that vacation can't come fast enough, and all she can think about is her school project."

Carole laughed. "That's just one of the things that makes Lisa Lisa."

"True," Stevie said, glancing again at Lisa, who had just reached her destination. "I guess—"

Carole never found out what Stevie was about to say, because her words were interrupted by Lisa's loud, horrified voice calling out their names.

WHEN CAROLE AND Stevie reached her side seconds later, they saw that Lisa's face was pale and her expression shocked. She didn't say a word. She simply pointed.

The land sloped away sharply on the far side of the hill. In the valley directly below the girls was a cluster of buildings that made up a small, ramshackle farm. Carole and Stevie hardly noticed the dilapidated farmhouse, barn, and other outbuildings. They immediately focused their attention on the source of Lisa's horror—a tiny, muddy corral with a horse in it.

Even from a distance it was obvious that there was something very wrong with the horse. It was painfully thin and standing with its head hanging low and one forefoot lifted off the ground. It was difficult to tell what color the horse was because its coat was matted and filthy. The horse clearly needed veterinary help—and fast.

"What should we do?" asked Stevie.

"I don't know," Carole said slowly. "We can't just leave the poor thing here."

"How bad off do you think it is?" Stevie asked.

"It's hard to tell from here," Carole said uncertainly.

"Maybe we should go down and take a quick look," Stevie suggested. "If the horse looks as bad from there as it looks from here, we can go get help."

Carole bit her lip. There was nothing she hated more than seeing an animal that was obviously in pain. But this horse was on private property and she wasn't sure what they should do. "If the owner of the farm is home, I'm not sure I want to meet him."

"That's a good point," Stevie said. "Lisa, what do you . . ." Her voice trailed off as she turned and saw that Lisa was already climbing down the steep slope, picking her way carefully among the slippery rocks and thornbushes. Carole and Stevie exchanged glances, then followed. Lisa was the most sensible member of The Saddle Club. If she thought they should go down to the horse, down they would go.

The Saddle Club approached the corral slowly, casting nervous glances at the nearby house. They could hear a dog barking inside. But there was no other sign of life or movement, and when they got a little closer, Carole noticed that there were several newspapers piled on the porch, still wrapped in the plastic bags in which they were delivered.

"It looks like whoever owns that poor horse hasn't been home for a few days at least," Carole said, pointing at the papers. She felt relieved and angry at the same time. She was relieved that the girls weren't likely to meet the owner of the farm, and she was angry that someone would leave a horse and a dog alone for several days.

By this time the girls were close enough to get a good look at the horse in the corral. It was a gray mare, though the sores and filth that covered her thin body made it difficult to tell what she might once have looked like. Her sides were crisscrossed with red welts and scratches, and the forefoot she was holding off the ground was badly swollen. It was obvious that her coat hadn't been clipped or brushed in a very long time, and her mane and tail were knotty and matted with debris. She had long, slender legs and a well-shaped head, but at the moment both were covered with cuts and sores. Her sides were bony from malnutrition, and her breathing was labored and a little too fast. Every few seconds a visible shudder would pass over her whole body.

"Wow," Stevie said grimly. Her friends didn't say a word for a few minutes. They were too shocked by what they saw to speak.

Finally Lisa broke the silence. "She looks even worse than Sal," she whispered.

It took Carole and Stevie a moment to realize what Lisa

was talking about. Then they remembered. Sal was a horse that had been rescued by a local animal welfare organization called the County Animal Rescue League, or CARL for short. He had been badly neglected and abused. Lisa had met Sal when she had visited the CARL facility. Despite the top-notch care he had received there, Sal's injuries had proved to be too much for him, and he had died not long after being rescued. The memory of the abused horse was something Lisa would never forget.

"She looks bad, all right," Carole said, staring at the mare, which hadn't reacted to their arrival at all. "In fact, I'd guess she's just about on her last legs. We've got to get help. Fast." She sometimes volunteered as an assistant to the local equine vet, Judy Barker. While making rounds with Judy, Carole had seen a number of abused animals. She knew immediate medical attention was the key factor in their recovery—though some, like Sal, were too far gone to save.

"There's only one thing to do," Stevie said. "Let's call CARL. This mare qualifies for a rescue if any animal ever did."

"I hate to leave her here," Lisa said, taking a step closer to the fence. At the movement, the mare raised her head for the first time and stared dully at the girls.

"Don't try to approach her," Carole advised gently. "We'd better leave that to the experts." She glanced at the farmhouse again. "I just hope whoever did this doesn't come back before the people from CARL get here."

"That doesn't seem too likely," Stevie said.

"No," Carole agreed. She glanced again at the empty house and shuddered. "Still, I wouldn't want to take any chances."

"Maybe I should stay here with her," Lisa said.

Stevie shook her head. "No way. If the horse's owners come back, I don't think you'd want to meet them alone."

"Right," Carole agreed. "Anyone who could do this to a horse probably wouldn't hesitate to do something just as horrible to you. We'd better hurry and find a phone."

"There's one in the visitors' center by the park entrance," Stevie said. She pulled out the map she had picked up at the visitors' center and studied it carefully. "If we take the Green Trail we'll get back much faster."

"Let's go," Carole said. She started to follow, then paused and glanced back at Lisa, who had lifted her camera and was pointing it at the mare. "Come on, Lisa," she called.

"Just a minute," Lisa replied. She could barely stand to look at the poor battered creature through the viewfinder, but she forced herself to use the last of the film photographing the horse. She had a feeling the pictures would come in handy.

Then she turned and followed her friends, glancing over her shoulder at the mare every few steps. The horse barely seemed aware of their retreat. Her head was hanging down once again, and her sunken sides moved visibly as she struggled to breathe.

"Hold on," Lisa whispered under her breath. "Please hold on. You'll be safe soon."

She just hoped it was true.

TWENTY MINUTES LATER the girls were on the phone with the volunteer receptionist at CARL, a young man named Nicholas Canfield. After taking down all the necessary information, he warned the girls not to go back to the farm.

"But we want to help," Lisa insisted.

"Are you sure about that?" Nicholas asked. "If the horse is as bad off as you say, there may not be much we can do. It might be easier if you weren't there in case we have to put her down."

Lisa didn't even want to think about that. "We want to help," she said again.

"All right then. Just wait at the park in the visitors' center," Nicholas said. "One of the cars will pick you up on the way back. But don't go near that farm yourselves."

"We won't," Lisa promised. "But please hurry."

As Lisa started to hang up, Carole took the phone and fished another quarter out of her pocket. "I want to call Judy," she said. "They might not call her until after they bring the horse back, and there's no time to lose. Besides, maybe we can prepare her for some of the problems."

14

"Good idea," Stevie said. "If anyone can help that horse, Judy can."

Carole reached the vet on the phone in her truck. With the other two girls helping her, she quickly told Judy everything she could remember about the mare's condition.

"Sounds bad," Judy said when they had finished, her voice strange and tinny on the portable phone. "I'm not far from CARL right now. I'll head over there and get ready to meet them when they return with the mare."

"We'll see you there," Carole promised, then hung up. After that, all the girls could do was wait.

IT SEEMED LIKE hours before one of the CARL volunteers arrived at the visitors' center to pick up The Saddle Club. The volunteer, a plump, friendly middle-aged woman with blond hair who introduced herself as Luanne Gregg, told them that the rescue had been successful and that the horse was on her way to the CARL facility.

"We took the police along in case of any trouble," she explained. "But the owner wasn't home. The cops stayed behind to wait." She paused. "I hope they'll be able to convince the owner to turn over that dog we heard inside the house, too. If the horse was treated this badly, it's a safe bet the dog isn't being properly cared for, either."

"I hope the police catch the owner soon," Lisa said forcefully. "I hope they throw the jerk in jail and throw away the key."

Luanne nodded. "I know, sweetie. It's hard to believe how cruel some people can be," she said. "That's why I like working with CARL. It makes me feel like I'm doing something important."

It wasn't far to the facility, which consisted of a redbrick building set on several acres dotted with runs and kennels. There was also a small corral where Sal had spent his final days and where the few other large animals CARL rescued were kept.

"It looks pretty crowded," Carole commented as Luanne pulled her car up to the CARL building. Most of the outdoor kennels were occupied, and there were several goats and a small flock of sheep in the corral. The sounds of barking and bleating filled the air.

"We have a full house, all right," Luanne said. "Those goats and sheep come from a small farm whose barn burned down last week. The owner is down on his luck and can't afford to board them, so we were called in to help him out until he can rebuild. We're glad to do it, of course, but it does make space a little tight."

"Look, that must be the mare now," Stevie said, pointing. A horse van was just turning into the driveway. Judy Barker's familiar pickup truck was already parked in front of the building.

The van stopped and the girls piled out of the car and watched Judy Barker and several other women, whom The Saddle Club recognized as CARL workers, coax the mare out. The horse was obviously nervous, shying as best she could in the narrow confines of the van. At last she seemed to tire from the fight, and Judy led her down the ramp into the grassy yard. Even then, the mare watched Judy nervously. When the vet reached up to stroke her head, the mare moved back a step.

"I guess she's afraid of people," Stevie said.

"Wouldn't you be if you were her?" Lisa asked. "I wonder where they're going to put her." She glanced at the corral, where the curious goats and sheep had moved toward the fence to watch the action in the yard.

The CARL volunteers held the mare while Judy checked her over. The examination seemed to take a long time. It took Judy several tries to lift each of the horse's feet, especially the swollen one, and the mare flinched every time she was touched. When Judy gave her a series of shots, the mare tossed her head and backed up. Another volunteer had to hurry forward to help keep her still.

"She doesn't seem violent or anything," Carole commented as she watched. "She's just trying to get away because she's scared."

"That's a good sign, isn't it?" Stevie said.

"I hope so," Carole said with a shrug.

Finally Judy stepped back, and one of the volunteers led

the mare to the paddock gate and released her inside. The sheep and goats came forward to sniff at her, but the horse ignored the other animals completely. Her head was hanging lower than ever, and she seemed completely exhausted.

Lisa left her friends by the paddock fence and hurried over to Judy, who was crouched down beside her truck, rummaging through her black medical bag. "How is she?" she asked the vet.

Judy stood up and looked down at Lisa, her expression grim. "Bad," she said. "About as bad as she can be. I've given her a tetanus shot and antibiotics, and some of the CARL people are already busy cooking up a hot bran mash for her. But those things won't be enough to do the trick. A lot of those cuts and welts are infected. She has a fever. Her right forefoot has an advanced case of thrush, and all three of her other feet are mildly infected as well. Considering the conditions she was kept in, I'd be amazed if she didn't have a bad case of worms. I'll have to give her a treatment for that, too. It won't be easy on her body, but it's got to be done. She doesn't look good, Lisa. Not good at all."

"Will she be all right now that she's being treated?" Lisa asked.

"I'm not sure," Judy said. "To tell you the truth, I almost think it might be kinder to put her down instead of letting her continue to suffer. She has a pretty slim chance of pulling through."

Lisa gasped. An image of Sal flashed into her mind. This

19

mare couldn't meet the same fate—she just couldn't. "No!" she exclaimed.

Judy put a hand on Lisa's shoulder. "Believe me, I understand how you feel," she said kindly. "But we have to be realistic. CARL has limited resources, and they have to use them on the animals that can be saved, not on those that can't."

Lisa glanced from Judy to the corral, where the mare was huddled against the far fence. The goats and sheep were milling around nearby. It didn't seem like the perfect recovery room. Suddenly Lisa had a brainstorm.

"What if we moved the mare to Pine Hollow?" she blurted out. "Max would probably agree to lend her a stall, wouldn't he? Maybe there she'd have a better chance of recovering. My friends and I could take care of her, and—"

"Hold on, Lisa," Judy interrupted. "I know you girls are hard workers, but this mare is going to need constant care for the next few days if she's even going to have a chance to pull through. I think she'll be better off here at CARL, where she can be monitored twenty-four hours a day."

Lisa was disappointed for a second. Then she realized what the vet had just said. "Does that mean you think she might pull through?" Lisa asked. "That she doesn't have to be put to sleep?" She held her breath while she waited for Judy's answer.

Judy watched the mare for a moment. Finally she spoke.

"I guess we can wait and see how it goes. She deserves at least a chance to make it."

Carole and Stevie joined them just in time to hear Judy's words. "Of course she does," Carole said. "And we're going to see that she gets the best chance she can."

Stevie nodded. "We just talked to Nicholas, that guy we spoke to on the phone," she told Lisa, pointing across the yard at a thin man with wire-rimmed glasses. "He said they'd welcome our help with the mare while she's here."

"Great," Lisa said. "Don't worry, Judy. We'll make you glad you didn't decide to put her down."

"What? Hold on a second. Who said anything about putting her down?" Stevie exclaimed.

"Relax, Stevie," Judy said. "Lisa already talked me out of it. We're not going to do anything drastic right now. But I want you to understand that this is a long shot. Only time will tell if she's going to recover. And if the CARL folks and I think she's suffering needlessly, we may have to put her down eventually, for her own sake."

"She'll recover," Stevie said with certainty. "We'll make sure she does. We can't let the animal abusers win this time."

"Not like with Sal," Lisa added quietly.

"Well, sometimes a positive attitude is the best medicine," Judy said with a shrug. "Come on, we'd better get started. You girls can help me clean out all those wounds, worm her, and pack her feet with thrush medication."

"Aye, aye, Captain," Carole said. "Just tell us what to do."

For the next half hour The Saddle Club worked hard, directed by Judy and watched by the goats and sheep. They cleaned and dressed the mare's wounds, brushed the worst of the dirt from her coat, and cleaned the infected feet so that Judy could pack the cavities with medicine.

Finally Judy stepped back and wiped her forehead with the back of one hand. "I think that's about it for right now," she said. "Good job, girls. Now all we can do is wait. If she makes it through the night, she just might have a fighting chance."

"How's it going out here?" asked Nicholas, appearing behind them with a large, steaming tub in his hands.

"Hard to say," Judy replied honestly. "We've got her cleaned up as best we can. Is that the bran mash?"

"Sure is," Nicholas replied. He set the tub down, then pulled a paper bag out of his pocket. Walking to the far side of the corral, he reached into the bag and pulled out a handful of what looked like corn kernels. He scattered the kernels inside the corral, and within seconds every goat and sheep in the place was greedily searching the ground for the tasty morsels.

Then he walked back to where Judy and girls were standing. "That should keep them busy for a few minutes," he said. "And keep their noses out of the big girl's food." He picked up the tub and set it down carefully just inside the gate. The horse's ears flicked in his direction and her nostrils flared. She shied away from Nicholas and let out a snort.

"Step back, everyone," Judy ordered. "Give her some space."

They moved around the outside of the corral so that the goats and sheep were between them and the mare. As Nicholas continued to toss handfuls of corn to distract the other animals, the horse cautiously sniffed at the aroma rising from the tub. Then, after much hesitation, she stepped forward, lowered her head to examine the tub's contents more closely, and finally started to eat.

When the mare had finished every drop of mash in the tub, Nicholas reached in and removed it. The mare shied away from him, returning to her spot on the far side of the corral. "That should help her," he commented with satisfaction.

Judy was more cautious. "At least she's eating," was all she would say.

Carole turned to Nicholas. "Have you heard anything about the owner?"

"I haven't," Nicholas said. "But maybe someone has. Let's go find out."

Judy nodded. "And I'd better find out who'll be watching the mare overnight and give them some instructions."

The group headed into the CARL building. While Judy went to the front desk to find out who would be on duty that night, the girls and Nicholas found Luanne in the dog room. She was brushing one of the inmates, a big, friendly mixed breed with long brown-and-white fur.

"How's the mare?" Luanne asked after greeting them.

"Judy has done all she can for her," Carole reported. "Now she says all we can do is wait and see."

"Did the police catch the creep who owns her?" Stevie asked.

Luanne shook her head. "Sorry, sweetie. They didn't. They waited around for an hour or so, then gave up and left a note. They're going to check back at the farm later, but they're afraid the owners might be out of town. If so, I just hope they left some food for that dog."

"Me too," Carole said. She was crazy about horses, but she loved other animals, too, and she hated to think that another creature might still be suffering on that terrible farm.

"Don't worry, they'll track the owner down sooner or later," Nicholas assured the girls, pushing his glasses farther up his nose.

"I hope it's sooner," Stevie said. She yawned. "Boy, am I tired. All that veterinary nursing is exhausting." She glanced at her friends. "I think we've done all we can do here for now. What do you say we call my dad to come pick us up? It's time to head back to my place and relax."

"Sounds good to me," Carole said.

Lisa shook her head. "You guys go ahead. I think I'll stay here for a while. Judy might need my help."

"But how will you get back to my house?" Stevie asked. "It's too far for you to walk. Maybe we should all stay."

"That's okay," Luanne put in. "I'm not leaving for another hour or so. If Lisa wants to stay, I can drop her off on my way home."

"Thanks, Luanne," Lisa said quickly, before her friends could protest any further. "That would be great. I'll see you guys in an hour then, okay?"

"Well, okay," Carole said. "If you're sure you want to stay."

"I'm sure," Lisa said firmly.

WHEN CAROLE AND Stevie walked into the Lakes' house with Stevie's father, the first person they saw was Alex.

"Well, if it isn't Romeo," Stevie commented. "Where's Juliet?"

Mr. Lake just smiled. "Take it easy, Stevie, okay?" he said. "By the way, you girls missed dinner. There's leftover chicken in the fridge and pizza in the freezer. Just help yourselves." With that, he disappeared upstairs.

"It's funny you should mention *Romeo and Juliet*, Stevie," Alex said with a smile. "Paige and I were just talking about it today in school. We might ask our teacher if we can act out one of the love scenes for our final English project next semester. We think we'd be perfectly cast as star-crossed lovers."

"Star-crossed *losers* is more like it," Stevie muttered.

25

Carole heard her, but she didn't think Alex did. He was gazing into space, a dreamy look in his eyes and an even dreamier smile on his face. He was also humming quietly. It took Carole a moment to place the tune, but finally she recognized it as a popular song called "You've Stolen My Heart."

Stevie obviously recognized it, too, because she let out a disgusted snort and stomped off toward the kitchen.

Carole followed. "You weren't kidding about Alex," she said as soon as they were out of earshot. "He has it bad."

"I told you," Stevie said. "Isn't it annoying? I've been waiting for the day when Alex finally found a girl who could stand him. I thought then I'd have a chance to get him back for all the times he's teased me about Phil. But now I can't even get him to pay attention long enough to make him mad." Phil Marsten was Stevie's boyfriend, who lived in a town a few miles away. Luckily he had sisters, so he understood when Stevie's brothers teased her about the relationship.

Carole laughed. "At least you're making a valiant effort," she comforted her friend. "And isn't that what counts?"

"I don't know," Stevie said. Finally she gave in and broke into a grin. "Okay, I guess you're right. Everything is more fun if it's a challenge."

The girls heated up a couple of slices of frozen pizza and headed for the living room. Alex was there watching TV.

"Am I seeing things?" Stevie asked, pretending to be sur-

26

prised. "Don't tell me you're staying home alone on a Saturday night—date night. Is there trouble in paradise?"

"Don't be ridiculous, Stevie," Alex replied. "Paige and I don't have to see each other *every* night. Our relationship is much stronger than that. Besides, she's visiting her grandmother tonight."

Stevie finished chewing a bite of pizza and shot Carole a sly look. "Hey, Alex, Carole was just asking me what Paige is like," she said innocently. "Why don't you tell her?"

Alex's face lit up. "She's great!" he said. "You'd really like her, Carole. I mean, everybody does. She's really pretty, and sweet, and she has a terrific sense of humor."

"No, no, Alex," Stevie said. "You must have misunderstood me. I asked you to tell her about *Paige*, not Belle." Belle was Stevie's horse. She was a sweet, pretty mare with a playful disposition.

"Ha, ha," Alex said with a frown. "I should have known you'd find a way to change the subject from the greatest girl in the world to your old nag. Now if you'll excuse me, this is Paige's and my favorite show. I promised I'd tell her all about it tomorrow." He slumped down in his chair and turned back to the TV, doing his best to ignore the girls.

Carole tried hard not to giggle. Alex really seemed to be just as obsessed as Stevie had described.

"Guess what happened yesterday in school," Stevie said to Carole.

Carole glanced up from her pizza, surprised by the sudden change in topic. "What?"

"I was taking an open-book quiz, and I couldn't find the answer to the first question anywhere," Stevie said. "Guess why?"

"Why?" Carole asked, more perplexed than ever. Normally the last thing Stevie liked to talk about was school quizzes, especially when she didn't know the answers.

Stevie grinned. "I was on the wrong *page*." She put special emphasis on the last word, and Alex looked up quickly from the television.

"What did you say?" he asked eagerly.

Stevie laughed, and this time Carole couldn't help joining in. Alex quickly realized what had happened, and his face turned red. "Laugh all you want, Stevie," he said stiffly. "It doesn't matter. Paige and I understand each other, and that's what counts. You obviously can't fathom that, so you might as well just leave me alone."

"All right, all right," Stevie said. "Don't go on a ram*page* or anything."

This time the girls' laughter was interrupted by the sound of the doorbell.

"That must be Lisa," Stevie said. She and Carole went to answer it, still chuckling.

As soon as they opened the door and saw Lisa's grim, tired face, they stopped laughing.

"How is she?" Carole asked immediately.

28

Lisa shrugged. "The same," she said wearily. "It's as if everything we've done for her has made no difference at all. She still looks awful."

Stevie put an arm around her friend's shoulders and drew her inside. "Don't worry, Lisa," she said. "Judy said it would take time, remember?"

"That's right," Carole put in. "Medical miracles don't happen in an evening, you know. You have to give her time to heal. With a safe place to recover and good people helping her, she'll get better. But Judy's right. It takes time."

"Sal had time," Lisa said. "He didn't get better."

Stevie and Carole exchanged glances. "We can't think like that," Stevie said sternly. "We have to believe in her. Otherwise, what's the point?"

Lisa didn't reply. She just shrugged again.

Stevie decided it was time to change the subject. "Carole and I were starving, so we already ate. Do you want a piece of pizza? I'll heat one up for you."

"No thanks," Lisa said. "I'm not really hungry."

Carole could tell that nothing they said was going to make Lisa feel better. It had been a long day, and they were all tired. "I don't know about you two, but I'm exhausted," she said. "Maybe we should just call it a day."

Stevie and Lisa agreed, and the three girls went upstairs and straight to bed.

LISA FELT A LITTLE better the next morning, and right after breakfast The Saddle Club headed to CARL to check on the mare. When Mrs. Lake dropped them off, the girls hurried over to the corral. The mare was there, standing in the middle of the small bleating herd of sheep and goats, her head hanging low. It was immediately clear to all three girls that her condition hadn't changed.

Carole bit her lip. "I hoped a good night's rest would help. But she doesn't look any better, does she?"

"Not really." Stevie paused as a dog started barking loudly from somewhere inside the CARL building. When the barking stopped, she continued. "And no wonder. Could you get a good night's rest around here? I wonder if it's this noisy at night."

Meanwhile Lisa was perched on the lowest rung of the corral's fence. The mare had lifted her head a fraction and was watching the girl suspiciously. When Lisa leaned forward a little, the horse shuffled back a few steps until she was pressed against the far fence.

Lisa hopped down from the fence and rejoined her friends. "She really distrusts people," she said. "That hasn't changed a bit, either."

"We've got to have a plan," Stevie said. "This definitely qualifies as a Saddle Club project. What can we do to help this mare get better?"

Lisa watched as a small black goat wandered by a little too close to the mare. The horse turned her head and nipped at it, sending it scurrying across the corral. "I think the first thing we have to do is convince Judy that the mare would be better off in a private stall at Pine Hollow, with us taking care of her," she said.

"What a great idea!" Stevie said.

Carole nodded, but before she could speak the girls heard footsteps approaching. They turned and saw Nicholas coming toward them from the direction of the CARL building.

"Hi," he greeted them. "You're here early today." He glanced at the mare. "Checking on the patient?" He leaned over the fence to get a better look. As he did, the mare tossed her head and skittered to one side, eyeing the young man nervously.

"Wow," Carole said. "She seems to like you even less than she likes us, if that's possible."

"I wonder . . . ," Stevie said thoughtfully.

"You wonder what?" Nicholas asked.

Stevie didn't answer for a second. Then she gestured to Carole. "Let's try something," she said. "Carole, why don't you walk around the corral toward the mare. Go slowly, and maybe talk to her a little. See how close you can get before she moves away."

"Why?" Carole asked, puzzled.

"I'll tell you in a minute," Stevie promised. "Just try it, okay?"

Carole sighed. At times like this it was usually easier to go along with what Stevie wanted than to try to figure out what she was up to. "Okay," she said. "Here I go."

Carole walked slowly around the corral. When she was sure the mare was watching her, she starting talking soothingly, trying to make her voice and her movements as non-threatening as possible. The mare eyed her nervously for a moment, looking uncertain about what to do. She jerked her head up once when one of the dogs started barking, but otherwise she didn't move. Finally, when Carole was only a couple of feet away, the horse took a step backward.

"That's enough, Carole," Stevie called. "Come back over here now." When Carole had rejoined the group, Stevie nodded to Nicholas. "Now you try."

"I think I see what you're getting at," Nicholas said, glancing at the mare, who had moved back to her spot against the fence once Carole had stepped away from her. "Let's see if it works."

Nicholas imitated Carole's movements, approaching the mare slowly and cautiously. But this time there was no mistaking the mare's reaction. As soon as the young man had taken a few steps toward her, the horse rolled her eyes fearfully and hurried away from him toward the center of the corral, the goats and sheep scattering before her.

"She really doesn't seem to like him, does she?" Carole commented.

Stevie waited for Nicholas to rejoin them before she answered. "It's not him she doesn't like," she said. "It's men."

Lisa looked skeptical. "Men?" she said. "What makes you think that? Maybe she just doesn't like the way Nicholas walks or something."

"Nope. I'm sure of it," Stevie said. "All the volunteers who were helping yesterday were women, remember? And the mare wasn't acting up too much during Judy's examination—well, not any more than you'd expect during something like that. But when Nicholas appeared with the bran mash she got a little wilder, remember?"

"You could be right," Carole said thoughtfully. "Maybe the person who abused her was a man, and now she's afraid of all men."

33

"It's a good theory," Nicholas said with a smile. "And it makes me feel less personally rejected. I'd hate to think this big girl just didn't like me."

"How does her condition seem to you?" Lisa asked. Stevie's theory was interesting, but Lisa didn't feel like discussing it any further. As far as she was concerned, they had more important things to worry about.

Nicholas pushed his glasses up on his nose. "Not too good, I'm afraid. It gets pretty noisy around here sometimes. I can't imagine she got a lot of rest overnight."

"That's what we thought," Stevie said. "Wouldn't it be nice if she had someplace nice and quiet and private to stay instead?"

"Sure," Nicholas said. "Unfortunately the local hospital doesn't admit horses as patients. And I don't think the country club would let her graze on the golf course. So she's going to have to make do."

Just then they all heard the sound of a vehicle turning into the driveway. They turned and saw that it was Judy's truck. The vet pulled to a stop, hopped out of the cab, and hurried over to join them, her eyes on the horse the whole time.

"Good morning, all," she said. At that moment the dog inside howled again, and the mare's head jerked nervously. A second later a car passing by on the road backfired, and the mare jumped. The sound also set the goats and sheep off into a chorus of bleats. Without another word, Judy returned to her truck and grabbed her phone. She dialed quickly as The Saddle Club traded glances. Who was Judy calling?

They found out a moment later. "Max?" Judy said into the phone. "Judy Barker here. Listen, I have a proposal for you . . ."

A HALF HOUR LATER Carole's horse, a handsome bay gelding named Starlight, watched curiously as his owner and her friends quickly lined the floor of an empty stall nearby with a soft bed of fresh straw and then filled the clean water bucket in one corner. For once, Carole had hardly more than a brief pat of welcome for him. She was too busy getting the stall ready for its new temporary occupant.

"That's it," Stevie said a few minutes later. "Everything's ready."

Lisa nodded. "Good. Judy and the van should be here any minute now."

As if on cue, the girls heard the faint sound of a heavy vehicle pulling into the stable yard. They hurried outside and saw the battered horse van from CARL with Luanne at the wheel. Judy's truck was pulling up nearby. Nicholas had stayed behind at CARL, since Judy had agreed that Stevie's theory about the mare's fear of men sounded plausible.

The girls walked forward to help as Luanne climbed out of the cab and started to swing open the back door of the van.

"Careful," Judy said, hurrying to join them. "We don't want to scare her with too many people." She pointed at

Carole and Stevie. "You two, go inside and ask everyone to clear out of sight for a few minutes. Then wait for us in the tack room. Lisa, you stay here and get ready to help."

The three girls did as she said. Stevie and Carole scurried away without a protest. Lisa felt calm and ready as she stood with Judy by the bottom of the ramp and waited for Luanne to bring the mare off the trailer. But when she heard the pounding of hooves on the inside walls, Lisa knew the horse was anything but calm.

"Don't move," Judy said to Lisa, moving forward to help Luanne.

Lisa couldn't see much of what was going on in the dim interior of the trailer. But she could hear the mare's nervous snorts, as well as the clanging of her hooves on the metal walls. The horse obviously didn't like being confined in the tiny space.

Somehow, between them, Judy and Luanne managed to calm the horse and back her slowly down the ramp.

"Lisa, you walk ahead of us," Judy said, keeping her voice quiet and calm so that it wouldn't upset the mare any further. "Make sure nobody's in our path who might startle her. Open the stall door, too, please."

Lisa nodded and obeyed. A few minutes later the horse was standing wearily at the back of the stall, keeping one eye on the humans watching her. Carole and Stevie had joined them, along with Max and Red O'Malley, the head

36

stable hand. The two men were standing back, trying not to upset the mare.

"It looks like she opened up a couple of those wounds again on her way over here," Judy said briskly after she had updated Max and Red on the mare's condition and treatment. "And her feet will have to be re-dressed daily, starting today. Any volunteers?"

Three eager ones stepped forward immediately. "Just tell us what to do," Stevie said, speaking for the whole Saddle Club.

"All right," Judy said. "But first you have to promise me one thing. This mare seems to like women and girls much better than she likes men, but she's still very nervous around all people, and who can blame her? It means you girls will have to be very careful when you're taking care of her— more so than you would be around any horse. Do I have your words on that?"

The three girls nodded.

"This is going to mean a lot of extra work for you three," Max told The Saddle Club. "If the mare won't let Red or me near her, you're going to have to be the ones to take care of her, at least until she settles down."

"We know," Stevie said. "We can handle it. And don't worry, we'll be careful."

"Good," Max put in. "I'll leave her to you girls, then. Call me if you need me. Come on, Red, we'd better get ready for the adult riding class. And I have a feeling that once we're out of sight, our guest will calm down a little." He hurried down the aisle with Red right behind him.

As Judy started to give the girls detailed instructions for taking care of the mare, Lisa listened carefully. But a small part of her mind wandered as she glanced at the horse in the stall behind them. The mare was still standing in the same spot, her head once again sagging tiredly as she stared at nothing in particular. She didn't even seem to notice the clean bedding and fresh water in her new home. In fact, her expression was no different than it had been when she was standing in CARL's crowded corral—or in her owner's soiled, muddy pen. Did she not notice the difference? Or did she just not care?

Lisa did her best to put such thoughts out of her mind and to concentrate on what Judy was saying. Once she was satisfied that the girls knew what they had to do, the vet excused herself to keep an appointment with another patient, promising to stop by later to check on the mare.

"Don't worry about a thing," Carole said as Judy got ready to leave. "The Saddle Club is on the case."

Judy nodded. "Call me immediately if her condition starts to deteriorate," she said. And, with that, she was gone.

"Nothing like a little optimism," Stevie muttered as the vet disappeared around the corner.

"You can't really blame her," Carole defended the vet. "She knows all the things that could still go wrong."

"Come on," Lisa said. Carole's words had brought the image of poor, doomed Sal into her mind, and she wanted to forget about that for now. She wasn't interested in discussing Judy's state of mind, either. She just wanted to get to work taking care of the mare. She grabbed the antibiotic ointment Judy had left for the cuts and sores on the horse's body. "Let's get started."

"THERE," STEVIE SAID an hour later, stepping back to admire her work. She had just finished applying fresh bandages to the worst of the cuts and scratches on the mare's legs. "That wasn't so bad, was it, girl?"

The mare ignored Stevie until she reached forward to stroke the horse's nose. Then the mare moved as far away as her cross-ties allowed.

"Don't worry, girl. We'll leave you alone for a while now," Carole reassured the mare. She slowly undid the cross-ties and set her free in her stall, reaching out to pat her on the neck as she did so. The horse shied away again and Carole's hand missed its mark.

Lisa sighed. "She's not getting used to us at all," she complained, a note of frustration in her voice.

"We have to be patient," Carole said, gathering the medical supplies and putting them in a bucket. "It takes a lot of repetition to teach a horse anything, and trust is no exception. Once she's sure we aren't going to hurt her, she'll come around." She paused, then added, "I hope."

"It's no wonder she's head shy," Stevie said. "If those marks on her back are any indication, she must have been beaten a lot. That would make any animal nervous around people, men or otherwise."

Carole nodded. "We're lucky she lets us touch her at all," she said. "Some horses probably wouldn't differentiate between us and men. They'd just avoid people altogether."

"I guess you're right," Lisa said. "But I wish we could let her know somehow that we're just trying to help."

"We are letting her know that just by being here," Carole assured her. "But we can't rush her. She'll trust us when she's ready. Right now the only important thing is that she gets well."

Stevie glanced at her watch. "I hate to nurse and run, but I'd better get over to Belle's stall. If she doesn't get some exercise soon, she's going to be just as hard to handle as this girl here." She paused. "By the way, it seems a little strange to just keep calling her 'girl.' Shouldn't we give her some kind of name?"

"I guess so." Carole avoided meeting her friends' gaze. "But I can't think of anything that fits right now, can you?"

"I don't know," Stevie said. "Lisa? What do you think?"

Lisa gazed at the horse, whose thin body seemed to sag as if it was difficult for her even to keep standing. "I can't think of anything right now, either," she said. "Maybe we should keep thinking about it until one of us has a good idea."

Carole nodded. She felt a little relieved to put off the decision for a while. As hard as it would be for all of them if the mare didn't pull through, it might make it even harder if they gave her a name. She guessed that her friends were both thinking the same thing, though neither of them said so out loud. "Okay, then," she said. "Starlight needs some exercise, too." She glanced at Stevie. "How about if we work him and Belle together in the ring?"

"Sounds good," Stevie said. "Lisa, do you want to come for a ride with us? I'm sure Prancer wouldn't mind a little exercise." Unlike Stevie and Carole, Lisa didn't have a horse of her own. Prancer, a spirited Thoroughbred mare, was the stable horse she usually rode.

"No, thanks. I'll stay here," Lisa said. For once she was glad not to have her own horse. It freed her to spend all of her time with the mare. "I'd like to try to do a little grooming if she'll let me. We got the worst of the filth off yesterday, but she's still pretty grimy. I'd like to see what color she really is under all that dirt."

"Okay," Stevie said. "We'll see you in a while, then." She and Carole headed for the tack room.

After they had gone, Lisa leaned on the half door of the stall, hoping that her presence would help the mare get used to people. But the mare seemed to be doing her best to ignore the girl. She stood at the back of the stall, facing the wall. Lisa tried talking gently to her, and for a moment the mare seemed to be listening. Her ears flicked back and her

41

head lifted a little. But then her neck drooped again and her ears went slack.

After standing and talking to her for another twenty minutes, Lisa decided it was time to try some grooming. Picking up her grooming bucket, she carefully slid open the stall door, talking quietly to the mare all the while. The mare watched Lisa warily as she entered the stall but allowed the girl to put her in cross-ties with a minimum of fuss.

"There, that's not so bad, is it?" Lisa murmured. She suspected that the mare's relative docility had more to do with exhaustion than anything else, but she didn't let herself think that way for very long. Instead she continued chatting while she wiped the mare's back and sides with a soft cloth, doing her best to avoid the worst cuts and abrasions. The mare flinched a few times when Lisa touched an injured spot, but otherwise she stood quietly. Still, Lisa could tell by the tenseness in the horse's body that she was far from relaxed.

Moving very slowly and carefully, Lisa ran the cloth down the horse's legs one by one, stopping well short of the swollen forefoot. She decided not to press her luck by working on the horse's face. That could wait for another day. Instead she picked up a soft body brush and carefully tried to work out some of the dirtiest spots from the mare's coat.

"Don't worry, girl," she said soothingly as she worked, moving the soft-bristled, wood-handled body brush over her bony sides. "This won't hurt a bit, I promise. I'm not even going to try to use a dandy brush on you until some of those cuts heal. But this will be enough to get you cleaned up a little. I bet you have a pretty gray coat underneath all this dirt, don't you?"

A few minutes later Lisa dropped the body brush into the bucket. "I guess you've had enough grooming for today," she said as she carefully released the mare from her cross-ties and shut the stall door. Then she leaned against the opposite wall and watched the horse for a few minutes. The mare's head drooped as she turned around to face the back of the stall. Within moments she looked just as she had for most of the time since Lisa had known her. The only difference was that this time a few patches of relatively clean coat peeked out from the mess of bandages and dirt that covered her. The clean spots shone gently in the dimness of the stall.

"I bet you were awfully pretty once," Lisa said in a low voice, talking more to herself than to the horse. "Silvery gray and beautiful." Lisa thought of Pepper, another gray she had known. Pepper had been her favorite horse to ride at Pine Hollow until his retirement. He had died of old age not too long ago, and sometimes Lisa still missed him. "It's hard to believe anybody could be coldhearted enough to let you get like this," she told the mare. At the thought, tears started to come to her eyes, and Lisa blinked them away quickly. This was no time to get weepy. She decided to go find Red and make sure he remembered that the mare needed special attention at feeding time.

When she returned to the gray mare's stall some time later, Lisa saw that the horse had turned around and was facing out. Approaching carefully, Lisa made sure to keep her voice low and unthreatening. "Hi, girl," she said. "Did you miss me?"

The mare pricked her ears toward her for a moment and didn't turn away as Lisa stood outside the stall. Still, Lisa couldn't help starting to feel sad again as she looked at the poor, pathetic creature. It seemed like such a long shot that the horse would ever recover completely from the terrible state the girls had found her in.

SEVERAL HOURS LATER Carole and Stevie found Lisa perched on a stool outside the mare's stall, reading a book about equine foot care. She had borrowed both the stool and the book from Max because she had wanted to read about thrush. She knew a little about it already—for instance, she knew that it was an infection of the frog, a part of the horse's foot, and that it was generally a sign of poor care, since it occurred when a horse's feet were allowed to remain wet or dirty for an extended period of time. But she'd never had to treat a case before and she wanted to make sure she knew exactly what she was doing.

"We're going to call it a day," Stevie said. "Are you ready to go?"

Lisa looked up from the book, marking her place with her finger. "You go ahead. I'm going to stay for a while."

Carole peered into the stall at the mare, who was standing in her usual position with her head drooping down tiredly. "How is she?"

"About the same," Lisa admitted. "She's definitely calmer here than she was at CARL. But her mood doesn't seem to have improved much otherwise."

"Too bad," Stevie said. "I guess I was hoping that just coming to Pine Hollow would make her feel better."

"Me too," Lisa said. "But when you've been through what she's been through, that kind of thing probably doesn't seem so important."

Carole nodded. "She's pretty far gone. We shouldn't expect too much, especially at first. Her recovery might be very slow."

"I just hope she starts to get better soon," Lisa said. She hesitated for a moment, then added, "I can't help wondering sometimes if she even *wants* to get better."

"I was wondering the same thing," said Carole, turning away from the stall to look at Lisa. "It seems like more than her body is broken. Her spirit is broken, too. And that can be much harder to treat."

"Well, we'll just have to find a way," Stevie said with determination.

Lisa sighed. "Once or twice today I thought there were little signs that she recognized me, but they were too subtle for me to be sure. And it doesn't seem to make her trust me any more than she did."

45

Carole squeezed Lisa's arm. "She'll come around," she said. But Lisa thought her friend didn't sound totally certain about that.

Carole and Stevie said good-bye to Lisa and left. Most of the other riders had also left, and the stable was quiet except for the sounds of horses settling down for the evening.

Lisa leaned back against the wall and returned to her book. But as she tried to read, her mind started to wander. She thought about what Carole had said about the mare's spirit being broken. It seemed to be true, and the thought disturbed Lisa. With Judy's guidance, Lisa was confident that she could do a good job taking care of the mare's physical ailments. But what if that wasn't enough? The best medical care in the world wouldn't make much of a difference if the patient had lost the will to live.

Lisa didn't know how long she'd been sitting there alone when she heard footsteps coming toward her from the direction of the entrance. It was Red O'Malley. "Lisa? There you are," he greeted her. "Your mother just called looking for you. She's wondering where you are."

"Oh, thanks, Red," Lisa said, glancing at her watch. "I'll call her back right away."

The groom nodded and hurried away. Lisa picked up the book and the stool and returned them to Max's office. Then she headed for the phone to call home. Unfortunately she wouldn't be able to come to the stable until after school the next day. Once again she found herself wishing that Christmas vacation would come quickly. This time it had nothing to do with the Starlight Ride—somehow that didn't seem nearly as important now—and everything to do with spending time with the sick mare. Lisa wanted to do all she could to help the mare get better. She just hoped that all she could do would be enough.

"ALL RIGHT, GIRLS. Line up in alphabetical order."

Lisa followed her gym teacher's order automatically, taking her place in line between Melissa Albright and Caitlin Avery. It was Monday, and the students were being tested in physical fitness. The boys were gathered on one side of the big gymnasium and the girls on the other. The teacher was telling the girls about the tests they would be taking. She was having some trouble getting her message across, since many of the girls were ignoring her and peeking across the gym at the boys, who were already warming up by doing push-ups. Lisa wasn't paying attention to any of it. She was too busy thinking about the sick mare.

She had called Pine Hollow first thing that morning. Max

had told her that the mare had had a restless night and seemed no better than yesterday. That wasn't the answer Lisa was hoping for.

She watched blankly as Sue Adams started doing sit-ups while the teacher counted. In her mind's eye she was looking over the edge of the hill in the state park at the bone-thin, miserable mare in the tiny, dirty pen below. It was an image she doubted she would ever forget—just as she would never forget the sight of poor Sal struggling through his final days in the corral at CARL. She remembered the way he had reached forward and gently taken a clump of grass from her hand. Even though his owners had left him to rot, he had still trusted humans, and there was something heartbreaking about that.

She hadn't been able to do anything to help Sal. But this time things would be different. Lisa was going to do everything she could to make sure of that. That morning she had given her father the roll of film she'd used on Saturday. He had promised to have the pictures developed that day and to stop by the police station to drop off copies of the ones Lisa had taken of the mare. Lisa hoped her photos would help the police to convict the mare's owner.

Her thoughts were interrupted when Melissa Albright nudged her in the ribs. "Hey, Lisa," Melissa said. "Did you hear who just asked Kimberly Poe to the Christmas dance at Fenton Hall?"

Lisa just shrugged. She really couldn't care less right now about who was taking Kimberly to the big holiday dance at Stevie's school.

But Melissa didn't seem to notice her disinterest. "Bobby Effingwell! Do you know him? He's the class president over there, but he's kind of a nerd. Still, Kimberly is excited about going."

"That's good," Lisa said with a sigh. "I've met Bobby. He's nice."

"He may be nice, but I wouldn't go with him," Melissa chattered on. "Hey, but speaking of Christmas, I heard that Mrs. Norton's homeroom class is chipping in to buy her a Christmas present. They're trying to get enough money to buy her a silver necklace to replace the one that fell down the drain when she was chasing that hamster around the science lab. Isn't that nice? My homeroom class would never do something like that, but that's because we have Mr. Ernst. We can't stand him—he never lets us talk after the first bell. What a grouch. I'd be surprised if he ever gets presents from anybody. So what are you getting for Christmas this year, Lisa?"

Lisa breathed a sigh of relief when the teacher finally called on Melissa to take her turn at sit-ups. Now she could go back to thinking about the mare.

But once the sit-up test was over and the group began the next activity—rope climbing—Lisa found herself standing near a cluster of girls discussing that Friday's performance of *The Nutcracker* in Washington.

A girl named Christy Marks noticed Lisa and drew her into the group. "Didn't you tell me that you're going to the ballet on Friday, too, Lisa?" she asked.

Lisa nodded halfheartedly. "My friend Stevie's parents are taking us."

"It should be great," commented a short, cheerful girl named Emma. "I don't like most ballets that much, but *The Nutcracker* is great. It makes everything seem so Christmassy!"

"No, I'll tell you what's Christmassy," Christy said. "It's hearing them play the same carols over and over again while you're shopping at the mall."

The other girls laughed, and Lisa did her best to pretend to join in.

Another girl, Amy Russo, finished her turn on the rope and joined the group. "What are you talking about?" she asked.

"What else? Christmas," said Emma.

"I can't wait for vacation to start," Amy said dreamily. "I'm going to spend the first three days sleeping. Then I'll spend the next three days at the mall. Then I'll probably just do nothing for the rest of the time. It'll be great."

"My parents are having a big formal holiday party on New Year's Eve," Christy confided. "My mom said I can wear a strapless dress if I can find one that's not too expensive. So that's my goal for the holidays."

As Lisa listened to the other girls talk, she began to wonder if everybody in the world had been infected with the Christmas bug except for her. She couldn't imagine getting excited about the holidays or stupid parties or strapless dresses. She had much more important things to think about.

She sighed as the teacher announced it was time to start the fifty-yard dash. It was turning out to be a very long day.

STEVIE'S DAY WAS going just as badly as Lisa's, but for a different reason. The reason was Alex.

It seemed that every time Stevie turned around, someone else was telling her about how ridiculous her twin was acting these days. One girl had stopped her in the hall to describe how Alex and Paige had held hands under their desks all through homeroom. Another had told Stevie about how Miss Fenton, the school's headmistress, had caught the couple smooching in the science lab. A third had spotted them feeding each other bites of cookie at lunchtime. And worst of all, every time Stevie spotted Alex herself, he had the dopey, lovesick expression on his face that she was quickly growing to hate.

"Stevie, you'll never guess what happened today in history class," exclaimed Patty Featherstone, catching up with Stevie in the hall between classes.

Stevie sighed. "Don't tell me," she muttered. She already knew that it was going to have something to do with Alex.

"Ms. Galloway caught your brother passing a mushy love note to Paige," Patty said with a grin. "She took it away from him and read it out loud in front of the entire class."

This was getting out of hand. Normally Stevie loved to see Alex humiliated, but normally she was the one humiliating him. The longer her brother's romance went on, the more eager he seemed to be to make a fool of himself at every opportunity. And Stevie was afraid it was starting to rub off on her.

She smiled weakly at Patty. "I'd better go. I don't want to be late for English," she said. She turned and headed down the hall. As she passed a group of kids standing by an open locker, they all turned to look at her. Then they turned back to the locker and started giggling. Stevie recognized some of them as members of Alex's history class, and she sighed. That must have been some note.

She had almost reached her English classroom when she saw them. Paige was standing against the wall, a pile of books by her feet and a single yellow flower in her hand. Stevie recognized the flower. Just that morning it had been happily growing from the orchid plant her mother had spent months coaxing into bloom. Stevie wondered if her mother had missed it yet. She had a feeling that when she did, Mrs. Lake was going to be very, very upset, but that pleasant thought would have to wait. Right now she had to try to talk some sense into her twin.

Alex didn't notice his sister approaching. He was leaning forward, his face only inches from Paige's, one hand against the wall by her shoulder. His other hand was brushing wisps of hair away from her face.

Stevie stopped behind him, her hands on her hips. She cleared her throat. She tapped her foot. They didn't notice.

Finally she decided it was time to stop being subtle. "Hey, lovebirds," she said loudly.

Alex glanced back at her over his shoulder. "Oh, hi, Stevie," he said.

"Hi, Stevie," Paige echoed. Then the couple returned their complete attention to each other. Paige tapped Alex on the nose with the flower, and they both giggled.

Stevie rolled her eyes. If they were upset about having their love note intercepted, they sure weren't showing it.

"Listen," Stevie said. "I just thought you two should know that everybody in school is talking about you. You're making complete idiots out of yourselves."

Alex didn't respond for a moment. Finally he glanced back at her again. "Sorry, Stevie," he said. "What did you just say?"

Stevie let out a loud, frustrated sigh. "Never mind." She stomped away to class, wishing that Christmas vacation would start right that second so she wouldn't have to put up with this humiliation any longer.

She spent the entire class period stewing about Alex and Paige. She wasn't sure how much more she could take of this. It was hard to believe that Alex had found yet another way to make Stevie's life miserable, but he had. Even the opportunity to tease him didn't make up for this. And if he and Paige were this annoying now, she couldn't imagine how horrible they would be after the big, romantic school dance on Friday. She just hoped that Paige would come to her senses before long and realize what a nerd Alex really was. Because if she and Alex didn't break up soon, Stevie was going to have to break both of their necks.

AFTER SCHOOL LISA found Carole waiting for her by her locker.

"I thought we could walk over to Pine Hollow together," Carole said.

Lisa just nodded and took her coat out of her locker.

Carole could tell her friend wasn't feeling any better about the mare. Carole had spent a lot of time worrying about their patient herself that day, and she wasn't feeling much more hopeful than Lisa looked. "I was thinking about the thrush, especially the bad case in that one forefoot," she said. "We could ask Judy if she thinks it would help to repack it more often than we've been doing. What do you think?"

"Sure, we could ask her," Lisa said. She pulled on her coat and grabbed the books she would need for her homework that evening. Lisa was very responsible about her school-work, and usually she liked to do her homework early to get it out of the way. But tonight she couldn't imagine when she would have time to get to it at all. "I don't think the thrush is the most serious problem, though."

"I know," Carole said. "But every little thing we can do to help will be a step in the right direction."

The two girls left the school building and headed toward Pine Hollow. Lisa was walking so fast that Carole had trouble keeping up with her.

"Hey, slow down," Carole said. "By the time we get there we'll be too exhausted to do any work at all."

"Sorry." Lisa slowed down a little. "I'm just eager to get there and see how she is."

"Me too," Carole said. "I hope a good night's sleep in a nice, quiet stable has helped her. Maybe if she's a little more relaxed today we could take her for a walk. Even though she's weak, it might do her good to stretch her legs a little."

"We can ask Judy about that, too," Lisa agreed. "Maybe getting outside in the fresh air will make her feel better."

"It couldn't hurt. And if her mood improves, I bet her health will, too," Carole said, shifting her backpack to the other shoulder as they walked down the sidewalk alongside a busy street.

"I think you're right." Lisa paused, looking thoughtful. "On the one hand, it doesn't make much sense that feeling sad would make a wound or a case of thrush heal more slowly. But on the other hand, it makes perfect sense. Actually, that's what scares me the most about the mare."

"What's that?"

Lisa paused to let a noisy truck go by before answering. "I'm afraid that if the mare doesn't really want to get better, she won't. No matter what we do."

"But if part of what we do is make her feel secure and wanted, that will make a difference," Carole argued. "All we have to do is make her see that life can be much better than it was with her last owner. Then she'll change her mind and want to get better, right?"

"I guess so," Lisa said. "But only if she changes her mind in time."

Carole could tell that the conversation was making her friend more depressed than ever. She decided to try to take her mind off it, at least for a few minutes. "By the way, have you decided what to wear on Friday?"

"I haven't really thought about it," Lisa said, reluctantly turning her thoughts away from the mare. She had a pretty good idea of why Carole had suddenly changed the subject, and she appreciated her friend's concern. "I guess I'll probably wear that blue dress I got in September."

"That would be nice," Carole said. By this time the girls had reached the outskirts of town. The sidewalk ended, and they left the road and cut across a bare field that adjoined

Pine Hollow's property. "I was thinking of wearing my green wool blazer, but then I thought I should save that for the Starlight Ride."

"You could wear it both places," Lisa suggested. Despite her worry about the mare, she couldn't help feeling a hint of anticipation when she thought about the upcoming events. She loved going to the ballet, especially when it was *The Nutcracker*. And the Starlight Ride was always special. She just hoped the mare would start to improve soon so that Lisa would be able to enjoy the events without worrying about her every minute. If not, she suspected that neither the ballet nor the Starlight Ride would be nearly as wonderful as usual.

As the girls continued to chat about *The Nutcracker* and the Starlight Ride, the familiar pastures and buildings of Pine Hollow came into view. Lisa's pace began to increase again without her realizing it. Now that she was almost there, she could hardly bear to wait another second to see how the mare was doing.

When they got inside, Carole offered to take Lisa's school things to the student locker room along with her own. Lisa accepted gratefully, and after handing over her coat and backpack, she headed straight for the mare's stall.

As she hurried down the aisle, she hardly noticed the friendly and curious heads of the other horses looking out at her. Her eyes were trained on one stall. Finally she reached it and swung back the upper part of the stall door, which was partially closed. When she saw what was inside, she gasped in shock, feeling as if she had just been punched hard in the stomach.

The stall was swept clean—and completely empty.

LISA JUST STARED at the empty stall for a moment, her mind racing. The floor had been swept clear of any scrap of straw, and the water bucket was clean and empty. It was as if no horse had been living there at all. Or at least as if no horse was living there anymore.

Lisa's heart started to pound so noisily that she could hardly hear herself think. What had happened? The mare hadn't looked good when Lisa had left the stable the night before, and Max had said her condition hadn't changed overnight. Had it all finally been too much for her? Had Max called Judy to put the horse out of her misery? Lisa had to know.

She raced toward Max's office, completely ignoring the rule against running in the stable. But Max wasn't behind his desk. Frantically, Lisa started searching for someone, anyone, to ask what had happened. She found Red O'Malley in the tack room.

As soon as Red turned around and saw Lisa's face, he guessed what she was thinking. "Don't worry, Lisa," he said immediately, dropping the bridle he was holding and hurrying over to her. "She's all right."

Lisa could hardly believe her ears. "Really? The mare? She's not . . ." Her voice trailed off.

Red shook his head. "I'm so sorry to have scared you," he said, placing a soothing hand on Lisa's shoulder. "It's all my fault. Judy came by earlier this afternoon and suggested we put the mare out in the paddock for a little while. Since it's not too cold today, she thought the fresh air and sunshine might do her some good. While she was out, I figured I'd give the stall a good cleaning. But I got called away before I could put the fresh bedding down, and I haven't had a chance to get back to it."

Lisa felt her whole body go limp. She collapsed on top of a trunk filled with spare bits. The mare was all right. She was still alive. "Which paddock is she in?" she asked.

"The little one in back by the garden shed," Red said.

"That's why we didn't see her when we came in," Lisa said, thinking aloud.

Red still looked contrite. "I'm really sorry I scared you like that, Lisa," he said. "I know how worried you are about that poor mare."

Lisa just shrugged. Now that the moment of panic was over, she wasn't interested in placing blame. She just wanted to see the mare. "I'm going to go check on her," she said.

"Okay," Red said. He picked up the bridle he had dropped and hung it in its accustomed spot on the wall. "Meantime I'll fetch some fresh straw and make up her bed. It's probably about time to bring her in. Judy said she'd be stopping by again soon to see how the patient is doing."

"Thanks." Lisa grabbed a spare lead line from its hook on the wall, left the tack room, and hurried outside, leaving through the back entrance this time. The mare was just where Red had said she would be, in the small, grassy paddock behind the stable building. Lisa called to her softly as she approached. The mare didn't turn her head, but she flicked one ear in Lisa's direction.

Despite her relief that the mare was still alive, Lisa couldn't help feeling a twinge of disappointment when she saw her. She was standing in the middle of the small paddock, seemingly unaware of the bright winter sunlight and the fresh, crisp air. Her head was hanging low as usual, and her scratched and battered body looked even worse in the sunshine than it had in the dimmer light of the stable building.

When Lisa let herself into the paddock, the mare raised her head a little and looked at her, her ears pitching forward. It was the strongest sign of interest Lisa had seen her take in anything so far, and she felt a surge of hope. The mare's ears drooped again almost immediately, but the hope Lisa had felt didn't fade entirely. The horse was in such bad shape that any sign of life was a good thing. Lisa stood near the horse for a few minutes, talking quietly to let her become accustomed to her presence. Then she clipped the lead line onto the mare's halter and gently, patiently, led her back inside.

The stall was made up as Red had promised, and Carole and Stevie were there waiting. Lisa smiled at her friends briefly, but she didn't speak to them until the mare was safely in the stall with the lower half of the door closed behind her. Then she quickly told them about her panic at finding the stall empty.

"We know," Carole said. "Red told us what happened. He feels really bad about it."

"It's not his fault," Lisa said. She sighed. "It's just that I keep waiting for the worst to happen."

"It's hard not to feel that way when she looks like that," Stevie said, gesturing at the mare, who had returned to her usual position near the back of the stall.

The girls leaned on the half door and silently gazed in at the mare. There didn't seem to be much more to say at the moment. They were still like that when Judy Barker arrived a few minutes later.

"How's she doing?" asked the vet, opening her bag and taking out her stethoscope, a thermometer, and some other items.

The girls stepped aside to let her look. "Not much better," Lisa admitted, half hoping that Judy would contradict her.

But instead Judy just nodded and let herself into the stall. She gave the mare a quick but thorough examination, paying careful attention to the lame forefoot.

When she emerged from the stall, she didn't look very happy. "Well, the thrush is starting to respond to the medication a little bit," she said. "But aside from that I don't see much improvement. The wounds are healing very slowly, and her temperature is on the high side. Plus Red told me earlier that she's not eating well. Of course it doesn't help that she pitches a fit every time he or Max has to come near her to feed her. You were right, Stevie. She really doesn't like men. Red had to hide around the corner when I led her out to the paddock earlier."

"What else can we do to help?" Lisa asked anxiously.

Judy shrugged. "Just hope," she said. "That's about all we can do for her at this point. Think good thoughts. And continue taking good care of her and monitoring her condition, of course."

"We'll do that," Carole promised for all of them.

"Good," Judy said. She started to pack her supplies back

in her battered black bag. "By the way, you girls might be interested in what the police told me today."

"Did they catch the owner?" Stevie asked.

"No," Judy said. "The man doesn't have a phone, so they can't contact him that way. They've sent officers out to the farm a few times, but he hasn't been at home."

"Maybe he moved or skipped town or something," Stevie suggested.

"They don't think so," Judy said. "They're pretty sure he's still living there. The mail's been taken in, and the officers saw fresh dog food set out in the kitchen—the CARL people made sure to have the police check for that. The problem is, the Willow Creek Police Department is so small that they don't have the manpower to stake out the farm for any length of time. Unfortunately other things are more of a priority."

Carole frowned at that. She couldn't imagine anything being more of a priority than capturing someone who would willingly hurt a horse.

Judy must have guessed what she was thinking. "Don't worry, Carole, they'll get him. And when they do, he'll pay for what he did. In the meantime, we shouldn't waste our energy worrying about it. Our job is to help this girl get better."

"You're right," Lisa said. She picked up the mare's water bucket, which needed refilling. "Let's get to work."

"That's the spirit," said Judy with a smile. She hurried off to look in at another Pine Hollow patient.

"I'd better go say hello to Belle before she forgets who I am," Stevie said. "I'll be back to help with the mare later."

"Okay," said Lisa. She headed for the water spigot. When she returned from filling the bucket, she passed Carole, who was carrying a pitchfork.

"Guess what," Carole said, rolling her eyes. "I'm on stall-mucking duty. Max's orders." Mucking out stalls was one of everybody's least favorite stable chores, but it had to be done. Max was strict about making sure everyone took her turn.

Lisa was glad it was Carole's turn today. That meant she wouldn't have to take time away from caring for the mare. After she had replaced the water bucket in the stall, she stood in the aisle for a moment staring at the horse. Remembering how the mare's ears had pricked forward in the paddock, Lisa wished the mare would make another sign to show that she really was still interested in being alive. But the mare stood perfectly still, head and ears down. The only sign of life was the overhead light gleaming on the clean patches of her coat.

Lisa decided to spend some time making those patches larger. She got her grooming bucket and put the mare in cross-ties. As usual the mare seemed wary about being handled, but she didn't object much this time. Lisa decided to take that as a good sign. She set to work.

After checking the mare's feet and brushing the outsides with hoof oil, Lisa decided to try cleaning the mare's head. She picked up the wooden body brush and held it up so the horse could see it.

"See? This won't hurt you," Lisa promised. Moving slowly and talking soothingly all the while, she ran the soft brush carefully over the mare's face and throat. The horse shuddered a few times but didn't move. After a few minutes Lisa dropped the body brush back into the bucket and took out a sponge. She dipped it in the water bucket and squeezed it out until it was just damp. Then she very carefully cleaned around the horse's eyes and nose.

"There, that's better, isn't it?" Lisa said. The horse didn't seem to respond to the sound of her voice one way or the other, but Lisa was used to talking to horses while she groomed them. She decided it certainly couldn't do any harm to keep talking now. "Your face looks nice and clean now. Maybe we can get the rest of you looking the same way." Before moving around to the horse's side, Lisa looked at her face one more time and sighed. The horse's face was clean all right, but the expression on it was still listless and disinterested. Lisa was beginning to wonder if the ear-flick in the paddock had been a fluke—or even a figment of her too-hopeful imagination.

She decided to stop thinking about that and get on with the grooming. She picked up a rub rag and started wiping down the mare's coat. Skipping the stiff dandy brush again, she went over the mare's entire body with the body brush, paying special attention to the dirtiest spots. As she worked, Lisa saw more and more spots of silver starting to gleam in the overhead light. The mare would really have a beautiful coat if she ever got better. It was a pale but very even silvery gray, which darkened only slightly on her legs and muzzle.

"You must have been quite the glamour girl once," Lisa told the horse. "A real star. Let's see what we can do with that mane and tail."

As she carefully worked the worst of the knots out of the mare's mane, which appeared to be the same shade of silver as the rest of her, Lisa pictured how the horse would look cleaned up and healthy.

"I bet you'd be the prettiest horse at Pine Hollow," Lisa commented aloud. Then, feeling slightly disloyal to Prancer, she added, "Well, one of the prettiest anyway." Thinking about Prancer made Lisa think about the upcoming Starlight Ride. And when she did, another thought occurred to her. "With that silvery coat, I just know you'd be a knockout under the moonlight on Christmas Eve," she said softly. "I wish you could be part of the Starlight Ride. Maybe I could even ride you. I'm sure Prancer would understand." Lisa felt a little foolish as soon as the words left her mouth, and she was glad no human ears had been around to hear her. There was no way the mare would be in any condition to be ridden in the Starlight Ride this year. And if the horse was to have any chance of seeing another Christmas Eve,

68

Lisa was going to have to stop dreaming about it and start working even harder to make it happen.

Shaking her head as if to dislodge any thoughts of Christmas and moonlight, Lisa stepped back to check on her handiwork. The mare might not look any healthier, but she certainly looked cleaner. As she gazed at the gleaming sections of silver coat, Lisa absently picked some stray hair out of the plastic mane comb she was holding. Her thoughts drifting, against her will, back to the Starlight Ride, Lisa didn't even notice when the mare's ears perked forward again and her dull eyes brightened just a little as she stared at the comb in Lisa's hand.

CAROLE WAS JUST finishing her cereal on Wednesday morning when the phone rang. Her father picked it up.

"Hello, Hanson residence," he said in his best military voice. He was a colonel in the Marine Corps. After listening for a moment, he broke into a grin. "That's easy," he said into the phone. *"The Grapes of Math."*

Carole knew that the strange comment meant it was Stevie on the other end of the phone. Stevie and Colonel Hanson were always trading corny old jokes, and most of them seemed to have something to do with grapes or elephants. Carole didn't even want to know what joke had elicited such a groaner of an answer.

She stood up and took the phone from her father. "Hi, Stevie," she said.

"Hi. How'd you know it was me?" Stevie said from the other end of the line. Without waiting for Carole to answer, she rushed on. "You'll never guess who's coming to dinner at my house tonight."

"Who?" Carole asked.

"Well, Lisa for one. And I hope you can come, too," Stevie said. "Because the guest of honor is none other than the wonderful, marvelous Paige Dempsey." She let out a mock groan. "You've got to come and shield me from the horror that is my brother's love life."

Carole laughed. "Sounds good to me," she said. "But if it's really going to be so horrible, why don't I ask my dad if you and Lisa can eat at my house tonight?"

"I already thought of that. My parents said no way," Stevie said glumly. "You'd think they'd be more understanding. After all, shouldn't it be enough that Alex and Paige torture me all day long at school? But they have no sympathy."

Carole quickly checked with her father, who gave his permission for her to eat dinner at the Lakes' house that night. "I'll be there," she promised Stevie.

"Good," Stevie replied. "My dad is making his world-famous lasagna, so at least the food will be good. If looking at Alex making goo-goo eyes at Paige doesn't make you lose your appetite, that is."

Carole laughed. "I don't know," she teased. "It takes a lot to make me lose my appetite."

71

* * *

LISA GLANCED AT the clock on the wall of her classroom, willing the hands to move forward more quickly. It was almost lunchtime, and she would finally be able to sit and think about the mare without having to pretend to pay attention. Usually science was one of her favorite classes because the teacher made it so interesting, but today Lisa could hardly concentrate as Ms. McCormick talked about the class projects the students would be handing in after the Christmas break. Since finding the mare on Saturday, Lisa had barely given a thought to her ecology project. Her father had brought home the developed pictures the evening before, but Lisa had hardly glanced at them before flipping to the ones she had taken of the mare. She knew she was going to have to get back to work on the project soon, but right now she could only concentrate on helping the mare get better.

Finally the bell rang and Lisa headed to the cafeteria. Carole was one grade below Lisa and had lunch at a different time, and Lisa didn't feel like talking to anybody else. No one else would understand about the mare. She found a seat by herself in the corner and did her best to eat her lunch, although she didn't really feel hungry.

As she chewed slowly, Lisa's mind was working quickly. In her head, she went over every injury and problem the mare had and tried to work out the best ways to deal with each one. The trouble was, the more she thought about it, the more certain she was that she and her friends were already doing everything they could. And still the mare wasn't getting better.

Once again, Lisa thought of Sal. She knew that the staff at CARL had done everything possible for him, yet Sal had died. His injuries had proved to be too much for any sort of medical treatment to cure.

At least Sal had seemed to take some comfort in spending his final days somewhere he felt safe and wanted. Lisa wasn't sure the mare felt the same way. She still hardly seemed to notice her surroundings, and, despite the moment in the paddock the day before, Lisa wasn't one hundred percent certain the mare even recognized her or her friends, or cared when they appeared or disappeared. In fact, she didn't seem to care much about anything at all. Was there any cure for that?

"IF ANYTHING WILL take your mind off the mare for a while, it's Alex," Stevie said as she, Lisa, and Carole entered the Lakes' house that evening. "This is sure to be a very interesting dinner. Disgusting, but interesting."

The three girls had just come from Pine Hollow. The gray mare was still no better, though today Lisa had thought she'd caught the horse watching her when she brought her a few flakes of fresh hay. The possible good sign had made Lisa even more reluctant than usual to leave the stable for dinner. But Stevie had finally managed to convince her that a dinner with Alex and Paige was an event not to be missed.

As the girls shut the front door behind them, they heard sounds of activity coming from the kitchen. When they entered the room a chaotic scene greeted them. Mr. Lake was standing with the oven door partially open, adding some spices to the contents, which smelled delicious. Mrs. Lake was at the counter mixing up a big bowl of salad. Stevie's younger brother, Michael, was running back and forth between the kitchen and the dining room, setting the table. After every trip back from the dining room, he paused to kick the leg of the kitchen chair where Alex was sitting. Paige was perched on Alex's knee. The couple was holding hands and gazing into one another's eyes. Alex's face as he looked at Paige held the adoring expression that had become familiar to everyone who knew him. Her expression as she gazed back was almost identical. Neither one of them seemed to notice Michael's kicks.

"Let me guess," Carole whispered as the girls surveyed the scene from the doorway. "That must be the famous Paige. Or should I say infamous?"

Just then Mrs. Lake turned around and saw them. "Oh, Stevie, there you are. Hello, girls. Could you three do me a favor and make some garlic bread? There's a loaf of French bread in the bin."

"Sure, Mrs. Lake," Lisa said. She couldn't resist sneaking

another glance at Alex and Paige as she walked over to the bread bin. Alex had reached up and was twirling a piece of Paige's hair around one finger.

Stevie walked over to the chair where Alex and Paige were sitting and smacked Alex on the shoulder. He looked up.

"What?" he asked. That was unusual. Normally if Stevie hit any of her brothers, they would immediately either hit her back or yell for their parents.

If Stevie was surprised at her brother's lack of retaliation, she didn't let it show. "Where are your manners? Aren't you going to introduce my friends to your little guest?"

"Oh," Alex said, glancing over at Carole and Lisa. "Okay. Paige, these are my sister's friends. Carole and, uh, Lisa. And this"—he put an arm proudly around his Paige's shoulders—"is my girlfriend, Paige Dempsey." He put a slight emphasis on the word *girlfriend*.

Carole and Lisa politely said hello. Paige just smiled at them and squeezed Alex's hand tighter. Then she and Alex returned their complete attention to each other.

"Well, so much for that," Stevie said, as the three girls left Alex and Paige to themselves and set to work making the garlic bread.

Lisa shook her head. "I must say, Stevie, I really thought you were exaggerating about them. But you weren't."

"Told you so. Where's Chad?" Stevie asked her father as she reached around him to grab the garlic powder.

"He's still at soccer practice," Mr. Lake replied. He closed the oven door and glanced at his watch. "He should be home in about twenty minutes—just in time to eat. He's bringing his friend David home to dinner."

Stevie didn't pay much attention to most of her older brother's soccer teammates, but she knew David. "You mean David Norfolk? He's the one who sings in that rock band, right?" she asked. She turned to Carole and Lisa. "This band is really cool, despite the fact that it's made up of a bunch of guys from Chad's class. It's called Rotting Meat."

Carole wrinkled her nose. "Ugh. What a name." She finished slicing and buttering the bread as Lisa prepared a pan and started laying the slices on it.

Stevie unscrewed the cap on the garlic powder. She sprinkled the contents liberally over the bread slices. Then, as Lisa carried the pan to the oven, Stevie glanced over her shoulder at Alex and Paige. With a sly smile, she carefully took a few steps toward them. When they didn't look up, she quickly reached over and sprinkled garlic powder over them.

"Stevie!" cried Mrs. Lake, turning away from the counter just in time to see what her daughter was doing.

Stevie looked sheepish. "Sorry, Mom. I couldn't resist."

To Carole's amazement, Alex and Paige hadn't even noticed what Stevie had done. Paige's nose wriggled a little, and she let out a tiny, polite sneeze.

"Gesundheit," Alex said, leaning over to grab a tissue out

76

of the box on the counter. He offered it to Paige gallantly, and she giggled and accepted, dabbing daintily at her nose.

Alex looked up and sniffed at the air. "Mmm, something smells good," he said. "I hope you put plenty of garlic on the garlic bread. I love garlic."

Stevie, Carole, and Lisa burst out laughing. Even Mrs. Lake couldn't help smiling a little. "Alex, could you do me a favor and get two of the folding chairs from the basement? We're going to be a big group tonight."

"Sure, Mom," Alex said, standing up. He took Paige by the hand. "Want to come help me?"

"Absolutely," Paige replied coyly. "Lead the way."

Stevie let out a sigh of relief when her brother and his girlfriend had left the room. "Is it just me, or did the saccharine level in this room just drop?" she commented.

"Let's lock them in the basement while they're down there getting the chairs," Michael suggested.

Stevie looked thoughtful for a moment. But before her parents could say anything, she shook her head. "No good, Michael," she said. "They'd probably like that. It would give them one more excuse to be alone together."

A few minutes later, Mr. Lake announced that the lasagna was ready. "Smells like the garlic bread is done, too," he added. "Let's eat!"

Mrs. Lake glanced out at the dining room table. "Would somebody please go tell Alex to hurry up with those chairs?"

"I'll go," Michael offered eagerly. He raced toward the

basement stairs. Standing at the top, he shouted at the top of his lungs, "Hey, Alex and Paige! Stop kissing and bring up those chairs!"

Alex and Paige appeared shortly, each slightly red-faced and each carrying a folding chair. "Sorry, Mr. and Mrs. Lake," Paige said. "Alex was just showing me, um, the basement."

At that, Stevie let out a snort of disbelief that even Alex couldn't help noticing. He shot her a dirty look, and Carole and Lisa giggled.

"That's quite all right, Paige," Mr. Lake said dryly. He glanced around and saw that his wife had finished bringing the food to the table. "It looks like we're ready to eat. Why don't we sit down and start on the salad. I'm sure Chad and his friend will be here soon."

The Lakes and their guests took their seats. Alex pulled out the chair beside his for Paige. Stevie watched him, then very theatrically pulled out one chair for Carole and another for Lisa. Alex and Paige didn't notice, but Michael did. He was already sitting, but he stood up and cleared his throat loudly. Stevie made a formal bow to him and then pulled out his chair, too.

"All right, that's enough, Stevie," Mrs. Lake said. "Carole, would you please pass the salad dressing?"

For the next few minutes most of the group ate their salads and chatted about the weather and the coming holidays, while two members of the group picked at their salads and gazed into one another's eyes. The only time they showed any other sign of life was when Mr. Lake asked them about the school dance. Alex spent several minutes telling everyone about the romantic way he had asked Paige to go with him, and then Paige spent the next few minutes describing how romantic the dance itself was going to be.

Then they all heard the sound of the back door slamming shut. A moment later Chad appeared in the doorway, mud on his face and a soccer ball under one arm. Behind him stood his friend David, a tall, athletic-looking boy with a shock of blond hair falling over one blue eye.

"Hi, everyone. Sorry we're late," Chad said. "Wow, the lasagna smells great."

"Go wash up, boys," Mrs. Lake said. "Don't worry, you didn't miss much. We just started eating."

A few minutes later the freshly scrubbed Chad and David were sitting at the table, helping themselves to generous portions of everything. Stevie introduced David to Carole and Lisa, then jerked a thumb at Alex and Paige.

"You already know Alex," she said. "That's his girlfriend, Paige."

David said hello to all of them, then turned to Stevie's parents. "Everything looks terrific, Mr. and Mrs. Lake," he said politely, reaching for a piece of garlic bread. "Boy, am I hungry. Soccer practice really works up the old appetite."

"What position do you play?" asked Michael.

"Forward," David replied.

"He's practically the star of the team," Chad added around a mouthful of salad. "The coach says he could have a future in soccer if he wants to."

"That's very impressive, David," Mr. Lake said.

David shrugged. "I guess it's cool. But I already know what I want to do when I grow up. I'm a musician."

"Tell them about Rotting Meat," Stevie urged. She turned to her parents. "They played at the last school dance, and they're really fantastic."

"Thanks, Stevie," David said with a grin. "It's nice to have fans."

Paige looked up. "Did you say you're in Rotting Meat?"

"It speaks," Stevie said under her breath so that only Carole and Lisa could hear her.

"That's right," David told Paige. "I'm the lead singer, and I play bass guitar."

"I thought I recognized you," Paige said, although Stevie would have sworn she hadn't even glanced at David until now.

"Hey, Paige," Alex broke in. He speared a piece of cucumber on the end of his fork and held it up. "I found another piece of cucumber for my little cucumber. Ready?"

"Of course," Paige replied. She opened her mouth, and Alex popped the fork into it.

Stevie rolled her eyes and turned back to David. "How come you guys aren't playing at the Christmas dance?" she asked. "I'm kind of glad you're not, since I'm not going. I mean I'd hate to miss it. But I'm surprised they didn't ask you back after the last dance."

"They did ask us," David said. "But we'd already booked a gig at a bowling alley over in Hazelton for the same night, so we had to pass."

"You guys must be awfully popular if you have to turn down jobs," Carole commented.

"Well, it's not like we're getting dozens of offers every weekend or anything," David said with a grin. "But I guess we're doing all right."

"He's just being modest," Paige put in. "Rotting Meat is the most popular band in town."

"Hey, Alex, would you please pass the pepper?" Stevie said. "I mean, would my little pepper please pass the pepper?"

Alex didn't seem to have heard her, so Michael reached around him and shoved the pepper mill toward Stevie.

Lisa helped herself to another piece of lasagna. "How long have you been in, uh, Rotting Meat?" she asked David.

"We got together last summer," he replied. "But it took a while for people to get to know us. Now we're finally starting to get some regular gigs."

"Where else do you play besides bowling alleys, David?" Mr. Lake asked.

"You played at the harvest festival over at the mall, didn't you?" Paige put in suddenly.

Stevie glanced at her, surprised that she was actually paying attention to the conversation.

Alex seemed surprised, too. "Hey, what are you guys talking about?" he asked.

"Your brother's friend is the lead singer of Rotting Meat," Paige explained.

"Are you a fan? Paige, isn't it?" David asked, smiling at her.

She nodded, smiling back shyly. "Totally. You guys are the coolest."

"You go to Fenton Hall, too, don't you?" David asked Paige. She nodded, still smiling.

Alex glanced from his girlfriend to David and back again. "Yeah, she's in my class," he said. He grabbed Paige's hand. "That dance where his band played was where we first got together, remember?"

Paige shrugged. "Well, we danced together a few times. But we really didn't get together until much later," she corrected him. She pulled her hand away and reached for her water glass.

Stevie kicked Lisa under the table. Then she kicked Carole. Something was going on here, and it was looking very interesting to Stevie. "So you're a huge fan of David's band, huh, Paige?" she asked innocently.

Paige blushed a little. "Well, I wouldn't say that," she said quickly, glancing at Alex. "But they're pretty good."

"Just pretty good?" Stevie said. "Or *really* good?"

"Shut up, Stevie," Alex said testily. "What difference does it make how good she thinks they are?"

"Oh, none at all," Stevie replied. "Not to me, anyway." She took a large mouthful of lasagna and chewed busily.

"That's enough, Stevie," Mr. Lake said warningly.

Stevie obeyed and kept quiet, but the warning was completely lost on Paige. She was gazing at David with the same look she had so recently directed at Alex. And he was gazing right back, smiling as he chewed his garlic bread.

Chad glanced from one to the other, looking dismayed. It was clear that he saw what was going on, too, and that he didn't like it. He turned to Carole. "So what's new at that stable of yours these days?" he asked loudly. "Any new horses or anything?"

Stevie could hardly keep herself from laughing out loud. When one of her brothers actually asked about Pine Hollow, she knew that something strange was going on. She was about to change the topic back to David's band, but Carole was quicker.

"Actually, there is one new horse there right now," she told Chad, shooting a look at Stevie. Alex looked so upset about what was happening between Paige and David that Carole felt a little sorry for him. She was glad Chad had decided to change the subject, and she was more than willing to help. "She's a gray mare we found who had been abused." She went on to tell them all about the sick mare.

For the rest of the meal the group discussed the mare,

Pine Hollow, and other topics. Stevie and her friends noticed that Alex kept shooting Paige sullen looks. They also noticed that Paige was ignoring the looks—if she noticed them at all. The only thing she was definitely noticing at the moment was David.

All in all, as Stevie told her friends later, it had been a very interesting meal—even more interesting than she could have hoped.

"You'll never guess what happened in school today," Stevie exclaimed when she found her friends at the mare's stall the next afternoon.

"What?" Carole asked, sounding distracted. She and Lisa had been checking on the mare and discussing the fact that she didn't look any better.

But Stevie had barely noticed the mare yet. She was too eager to share her news. "It's Alex and Paige," she announced. "They're Splitsville!"

"Oh, that's too bad," Lisa said, leaning against the pitchfork she had brought to muck out the mare's stall.

"Too bad, nothing," Stevie said. "This is great. It's exactly what Alex deserves for being such an annoying sap about the whole thing."

Carole didn't think that was a very nice thing for Stevie to say, but she decided not to mention it right then. Stevie had that look on her face that meant she was already dreaming up new ways to torture her brother. "What happened?" she asked instead.

"Paige dumped him like a load of old bricks," Stevie said gleefully. "She was so impressed with Chad's friend David last night that she's skipping the dance tomorrow so she can go to the Rotting Meat show at the bowling alley."

"Oh, poor Alex," Lisa said softly. "He was looking forward to it so much."

"Well, I guess he should have found a girlfriend who doesn't have a thing for older men," Stevie said.

"How is he taking it?" Carole asked.

"Let me put it to you this way," Stevie said. "I ran into him outside of school today when I was getting ready to come over here, and I offered to let him come with me. You know, I thought he might find someone to replace Paige at Pine Hollow. After all, Penny is pretty cute, and everyone knows Delilah is a real beauty, and then there's Prancer—athletic yet feminine."

Carole rolled her eyes. Penny, Delilah, and Prancer were all Pine Hollow mares. "Very funny," she commented.

"Well, I guess Alex didn't get the joke," Stevie said. "I don't think he even heard me talk about the mares. Because I would swear he was about to accept my offer and come here with me. Can you believe that?"

Her friends had to admit that that was more than a little bit strange. They knew that Pine Hollow was the last place any of Stevie's brothers would want to go.

"That just shows how upset he is," Lisa said.

"I know," Stevie said with a grin. "Can you believe it? Who would have thought my very own twin would turn out to be such a fool for love?"

Finally Stevie seemed to realize where they were. She glanced in at the mare. "Oh. How is she?"

"Not so good," Carole admitted. "I don't see much difference in her condition, although she did look at us when we arrived today. I think she recognizes us, even if she doesn't always show it."

"That's a good sign," Lisa said. She looked at the mare and sighed. The mare wasn't looking back at them now. "But it's a small one. She still doesn't seem to care much whether we're around or not."

"I already checked on Starlight, so I'll help you with the stall if you want," Carole offered. With that, the girls got to work.

Carole and Stevie worked hard, but Lisa worked even harder. She was such a whirlwind of activity that it made Carole and Stevie tired just to watch her. First she turned the mare out in the paddock and helped Carole muck out the stall. Then she cleaned out the water bucket and the hayrack and refilled them. Then she brought the mare back in, changed all her bandages, and repacked her feet with the thrush medicine. After that she gave her a complete grooming from head to toe until the silvery gray coat was more clean than dirty and the mare's mane and tail were smooth and tangle free.

"She must have been really pretty before all this happened to her," Stevie commented later as she and Carole leaned over the stall door and watched Lisa fix a bandage that had come loose during the grooming.

Lisa nodded. "I still can't believe someone could be so cruel to any animal, let alone such a gorgeous little horse," she said. "I mean, I know it happens. Just look at poor Sal. But it shouldn't."

"It's not right," Carole agreed. "That's why it's important for the police to catch that man and see that he's properly punished."

"I called the police this morning before school," Lisa said. "They still hadn't found him, but they said they were going to try to send someone out to the farm again today."

"Let's call now and see if they got him," Stevie suggested.

The other girls agreed. Lisa gave the mare a pat and let herself out of the stall, then led the way to the pay phone in the hallway. Carole fished a quarter out of her jeans pocket and dropped it into the phone, and Lisa dialed the number for the Willow Creek police station. By now she knew it by heart.

The sergeant who answered was the same one Lisa had spoken to that morning.

"Sorry," he said when he found out why the girls were calling. "We were hoping to get out there today, like I told you earlier. But we've been so busy around here we didn't have the chance. People tend to go a little crazy around the holidays—it's usually our busiest time. Today we had three car accidents, a bar brawl, and half a dozen shoplifters to deal with. And since we have no way of knowing when that fellow will be at home, it's a waste of time and manpower to keep sending officers out there when we need them here in town."

"But you've got to catch him," Lisa protested.

"Oh, we will," the sergeant reassured her. "Don't you worry about that. But it may have to wait until after Christmas when things quiet down a little."

Lisa thanked the officer for the update and hung up. She told her friends what he had said. "After Christmas?" she said as the girls drifted back toward the mare's stall. "That's weeks away."

Stevie nodded. "I hate to think of that jerk walking around like nothing happened after what he did. It will be hard to enjoy Christmas as much just knowing that he's out there."

"I just hope he remembers to keep feeding his dog," Carole put in.

Lisa nodded. "I know. I was thinking about that last night. We heard the dog barking when we were there, remember? For all we know, he could have a whole bunch of other animals that he's treating just as badly as he treated the mare. What a horrible thought!"

They had reached the stall by now, and they leaned on the half door and looked in. The mare stood dejectedly at the back of the stall, looking much cleaner than when they had first found her, but not much happier.

Finally Stevie stood up straight and looked at her friends. "We can't wait until after Christmas."

"I was just about to say the exact same thing," Lisa said.

"But what can we do?" Carole asked. "The police already told us they don't have time to go out there."

"That's because they don't know whether he'll be at home or not," Stevie pointed out. "I'm sure they wouldn't mind going out right away if they knew he was there, would they?"

"I guess not," Carole admitted. She looked at her watch. "But if you're suggesting we go over there ourselves and see if he's home, you're crazy."

Stevie looked hurt. "What do you mean?"

"I mean look at the time," Carole said, for a moment sounding almost as sensible as Lisa usually did. "We'd have to take the bus from the shopping center over to the park, and then hike along the highway—in the dark, I might add—for a couple of miles." She shrugged. "We can't do it."

"Well, how about tomorrow, then?" Lisa suggested, glancing at the mare, who hadn't moved. "We could go right after school, before it gets dark."

"Tomorrow's the ballet, remember?" Carole said. "We could do it on Saturday, I guess. But to tell you the truth, I'm not too crazy about going near that man's property. I certainly wouldn't want to meet him face to face without someone official around."

Stevie had a very thoughtful look on her face. "No, I think we definitely need to go tonight," she said. "And I know just the official guy who can drive us."

"Who?" Carole said suspiciously. When Stevie got that look, it usually meant things were going to happen. Sometimes they were good things, and sometimes they were bad things. With Stevie, there was no predicting.

Stevie smiled at her. "Your father, of course. If we can't get the police to go with us, we'll take the Marines."

A few minutes later it was settled. Carole had called her father and then put Stevie on the phone. It had taken all of her powers of persuasion, but Stevie had finally convinced the colonel to drive them over to have a look at the farm after dinner.

"We're not actually going to go near the house," he warned Stevie. "We'll just see if the lights are on, and if they are we'll turn around immediately and find the nearest phone to call the police."

"That's all we want," Stevie promised.

IT WASN'T EASY for Carole and Stevie to get Lisa to leave the stable early that evening. But after they had reminded her a few times of the reason, she gave in and went home for dinner.

She was already outside waiting, her arms wrapped around her body for warmth, when the Hansons' station wagon pulled into her driveway an hour and a half later. Carole was in the front seat with her father. Stevie was in the back.

"Hi, Colonel Hanson," Lisa said as she climbed in beside Stevie. "Thanks for driving us."

"Hi, Lisa," Carole's father replied. "As I was just telling Carole and Stevie, I'm not at all sure this is a good idea." He shook his head. "I don't know how I let you girls talk me into these schemes."

Stevie knew the "you girls" was directed mostly at her. She decided it was time for a change of subject before the colonel had a change of heart. "So who wants to hear the latest report on the lovelorn and lonely hearted?"

"I assume you're referring to your poor brother," Carole said, twisting around as far as her seat belt would allow to talk to her friends.

"Of course," Stevie said. She grinned. "If our errand here weren't so important, I would have hated to leave my house tonight. Dinner was fun."

"Uh-oh," Lisa said. "What did you do to him?"

"It wasn't just me," Stevie informed her. "Michael was helping. It's not often that I get to team up with one of my brothers against another one. Usually it's them teaming up against me."

Carole laughed. She knew that was no exaggeration. "What about Chad? Didn't he help, too?"

"No. I guess he feels sort of responsible for what happened," Stevie said. "He didn't tease Alex at all. In fact, he offered to punch David in the nose if Alex wanted him to."

Colonel Hanson chuckled. "That's what I call brotherly love," he said.

"Whatever it is, it didn't hold Michael back," Stevie said with a grin. "It was his idea for us to sing 'Heartbreak Hotel' while we set the table."

"Oh, that's mean," Colonel Hanson said. But then he

began humming the song under his breath. Carole knew it was one of his favorites—he loved all music from the fifties and sixties, and that definitely included all of Elvis Presley's hits.

Lisa had turned to watch the scenery pass as they drove. Now she turned back to her friends. "Colonel Hanson is right," she said. "You really should give Alex a break, Stevie. As annoying as he and Paige might have been, I'm sure he's hurting right now. And he is your brother."

"Don't remind me," Stevie said, rolling her eyes. "All of Fenton Hall can't seem to forget it. Anyway, you should have been there tonight. Mom and Dad made us stop singing as soon as they realized what we were doing. But it's amazing how many different ways it's possible to work the word *page* into a conversation."

She continued to describe the teasing Alex had received until they turned off the highway onto the road that ran past the farm.

"We're almost there," Carole told her father. "It's up about two or three miles on the left."

After that there was silence as the car approached the mare's former home. Lisa gripped her armrest so tightly that her fingers were white. Now that they were close, the trip didn't seem like such a good idea. She hated the thought of driving past the home of the man who had been so cruel to the gray mare. But she knew it was necessary. They had to help bring him to justice if they could.

Colonel Hanson slowed the car a little as they came around a curve in the road. The driveway to the farm was just ahead. Even before they reached it, they knew the owner was at home. The house was set back from the road, but every light in the place seemed to be ablaze and a battered pickup truck was parked in the driveway.

"He's there," Carole whispered.

Colonel Hanson nodded grimly. "All right. There was a gas station off the highway a few miles back. We'll call the police from there." He pulled into the driveway just far enough to turn around. As the car's headlights swung around, Lisa caught a flash of movement in the overgrown grass beside the road.

"Wait! Stop!" she cried.

"What is it?" Colonel Hanson asked, slamming on the brakes.

"I saw something," Lisa said. "It looked like an animal."

"What was it?" Stevie asked, leaning over to look out Lisa's window. "A rabbit or something?"

Lisa shook her head. "Too big." She peered out at the grassy embankment, willing her eyes to see through the darkness. Suddenly she saw the movement again. "There!" she cried, pointing as the animal stumbled into the range of the headlight beams.

"It looks like a dog," Carole said.

"Not a dog—a puppy," Stevie corrected. "And I think he's hurt."

The puppy cringed, blinking in the light, as Stevie threw open her door.

"Stevie! Stop right there," Colonel Hanson called in his most commanding voice.

Stevie froze with one leg halfway out of the car. "But we've got to help him."

"You know better than that. If he's hurt and frightened, he could lash out and bite you," Colonel Hanson said.

"But we can't just leave him here, Dad," Carole protested. "He might have been hit by a car. He could die if we don't help him."

"I didn't say we should leave him here," Colonel Hanson told his daughter gently. "You girls wait here. And I mean it." He unhooked his seat belt and put the car into neutral. Then he grabbed a pair of heavy work gloves out of the glove compartment and pulled them on. The puppy didn't move as the colonel got out of the car. It just crouched there, watching him.

Colonel Hanson stood by the car for a moment, watching the puppy carefully. The puppy continued to watch him. Then it let out a little whine and tentatively wagged its tail. The colonel whistled softly, and the puppy's tail wagged harder. It started to run to him but stumbled and fell.

"Oh, look," Lisa breathed. "His leg is hurt."

The puppy stood up again, managing to retain its balance this time. As soon as he was sure the animal wasn't aggressive, Colonel Hanson knelt beside the puppy, blocking the girls' view.

Stevie bounced up and down impatiently. "What's he doing?"

"He's probably checking to see what's wrong with him," Carole guessed. She stared at her father's back, trying to be patient. It wasn't easy.

When Colonel Hanson stood up and turned around a minute later, the puppy was in his arms. He walked around to Stevie's door, which was still slightly ajar.

"Could one of you girls help me with the back door?" he said.

Stevie jumped out and ran around to the back of the car. She swung open the door and then reached forward to help with the puppy.

"Be careful of his left hind leg," Colonel Hanson warned. "I think it might be broken."

Stevie nodded and crawled into the back of the car. The puppy's fur felt cold as Colonel Hanson slid him into the back of the station wagon to Stevie, though his tongue felt warm when he licked her hand.

"He must have been outside for a long time," Stevie said, scratching behind the puppy's ears after they had gently set him down on a pile of old newspapers.

Colonel Hanson nodded. "He'll be lucky if he doesn't come down with something. It's pretty cold out tonight."

Carole and Lisa had turned around and were watching over the backs of their seats. "Do you think he got hit by a car?" Lisa asked.

"Possibly, but I doubt it," Colonel Hanson said grimly. "It looks more like he was beaten, or possibly kicked."

Lisa gasped, and her gaze involuntarily turned toward the house lighting up the other end of the driveway. "You mean you think that man owns this puppy, too?"

"We shouldn't jump to any conclusions," Colonel Hanson said. "But if I had to take a guess, that would be it." He glanced at the house. "Come on, we'd better get moving before someone notices us out here and comes to investigate."

The puppy was obviously excited about all the attention he was receiving, and he wriggled eagerly and tried to follow as Stevie started to crawl out of the car.

"No, no," she warned, shaking a finger at him. "You have to stay still. You don't want to make your leg any worse than it is."

The puppy followed her finger with his head, trying to lick it. Stevie giggled.

"Coming, Stevie?" Colonel Hanson prompted.

"I think I'd better stay back here with the puppy," Stevie said, peering out at Colonel Hanson. "I'll keep him calm while we drive. Otherwise he'll just wriggle around and hurt his leg even more."

Colonel Hanson hesitated, then nodded. "All right,"

he said. "Just this once. Although I hate the thought that you won't be wearing a seat belt. What would your parents say?"

"Don't worry," Stevie assured him as she climbed in. "Just think of it as being like driving a horse trailer. The horses don't wear seat belts, do they?"

Colonel Hanson rolled his eyes, but he didn't say another word. He closed the back door and walked around to the driver's seat. Less than a minute later they were back on the road, heading for the highway.

"I guess we should take that poor pup over to your friends at CARL," Colonel Hanson said, once they had left the farm behind them.

"Where else?" Carole replied. "I just hope they forgive us for breaking their rule about leaving the rescuing to the experts."

"They've got to," Lisa said. "If we'd left him there, he would have frozen to death."

"I'm sure they won't mind this time," Colonel Hanson said. "But when we stop to call the police, we'd better give CARL a call, too, so they'll know we're coming."

It only took a few minutes to get to the gas station. After placing both calls, they got back on the road and didn't stop again until they reached CARL.

Nicholas was waiting for them when they pulled in. He hurried forward as Colonel Hanson and the girls got out of the car.

"I hear you brought us a patient," he said after introducing himself to Colonel Hanson.

"That's right," Colonel Hanson replied, leading Nicholas to the back of the station wagon. With Stevie's help, the two men soon had the dog out of the car and into CARL's veterinary examining room.

"I called Doc Tock," Nicholas said. "She should be here soon." The girls knew that he was referring to Dr. Takamura, a small-animal specialist who lived nearby. The Saddle Club had met her many times, partly because her daughter Corey rode at Pine Hollow and partly because she had taken care of their own cats and dogs. The girls knew that Judy could have cared for the injured puppy in a pinch, but she was primarily an equine vet. They were glad the puppy would have the care of a specialist.

The vet arrived a few minutes later. She gave the puppy a quick look and then shooed everyone out of the examining room. "This doesn't look too serious," she said, "but I need some room to work. You can come back in and see him after his leg is set."

Nicholas led the girls and Colonel Hanson out into the reception area. "That puppy's in good hands now," he commented.

Lisa nodded. "I'm glad he isn't hurt too badly," she said, thinking of the mare. "He's lucky."

While they waited, the girls filled Nicholas in on the

errand that had led them to find the puppy. "We asked the police to call us here when they caught the guy," Carole said.

"Good," Nicholas said. "Maybe then we can go out to that farm and make sure there aren't any other hurt animals there."

While they waited, The Saddle Club and Colonel Hanson went into the dog and cat rooms to visit the animals there. Seeing all the healthy, well-fed residents, Lisa felt both happy and sad. She was happy because it reminded her that groups like CARL managed to do a lot of good for a lot of animals, even if some, like Sal, didn't make it. But it also made her sad to think that so many nice cats and dogs were still without good homes. She told her friends what she was thinking.

"I know what you mean," Carole said, poking her fingers into one of the pens to pet a friendly black cat. The cat reminded her a little of her own black cat, Snowball. "But that should make us feel even better about bringing the gray mare to Pine Hollow. It lets her know what a really good home is like."

Stevie agreed. "And remember, CARL puts a lot of effort into finding homes for all these guys, too." She waved an arm to encompass all of the animals in the room.

Just then Nicholas stuck his head in through the doorway. "The police are on the phone. Who wants to talk to them?"

The girls raced for the phone. Lisa took the receiver Nicholas handed her and held it a little way from her ear so that her friends could listen, too. "Hello?" she said.

The same sergeant was on the other end of the line. "Hi there," he said. Lisa thought he sounded a little tired, and then she realized that he must have been on duty since she had first spoken to him early that morning. No wonder he kept talking about how short-staffed the department was.

"Did you catch that guy?" Stevie called out, hoping the officer could hear her.

"Uh, yes, we did," he replied, sounding a little confused by the new voice. "A couple of officers went out there after your call, and they just got back here with him a few minutes ago. He confessed to the animal abuse, thanks to those photos you gave us."

"Really?" Lisa said. "I'm glad they helped. Do you know if he was the owner of the puppy we found, too?" They had told the police about the puppy earlier.

"Is it a black-and-white shepherd mix?" the officer asked.

"Yes, I think so," Lisa said. "I mean, he's black and white. And he's got a lot of fur."

"That'd be the one," the sergeant said. "But I haven't even told you the best part yet."

"What's that?" Lisa asked, and Carole and Stevie leaned in closer, not wanting to miss a word.

"It turns out the guy has a record as long as Willow

Creek," the police officer said. "He was living under an assumed name out there at that farm, and that's why we didn't know it until now. But we ran his fingerprints through the computer and found out he's wanted for burglary in North Carolina. So not only will he have to pay a hefty fine for the charges we have against him here, but chances are he'll be serving some time in a North Carolina jail as well."

"That's great," Lisa said. Even though it didn't really help the mare any, Lisa was glad the man had been caught. And she was even more glad that he was going to be sent away. She hoped the North Carolina police put him in jail for a long, long time.

The girls thanked the officer and hung up. When they turned around, they noticed that Nicholas was pulling on his coat.

"Are you leaving?" Stevie asked.

"I'm going back out to that farm," Nicholas said. "That guy told the police about a few other animals he had. There's a goat, another dog, and a couple of chickens."

Two more CARL workers entered and grabbed their coats from the closet near the door. Nicholas took a set of keys off a hook behind the reception desk. At the same moment Dr. Takamura came out of the examining room.

"What's up?" she asked immediately.

"Rescue," Nicholas replied. "The same farm where the puppy was picked up."

"I'll come with you," the vet said. "Let me get my bag." She hurried back into the examining room and reappeared a few seconds later, carrying her leather medical bag.

"How's the puppy?" asked Carole.

Dr. Takamura smiled at her. "He'll be just fine. I gave him a shot so he'll sleep, but you can go take a peek at him if you want. One of the volunteers is getting a pen ready for him."

Stevie knew better than to ask if they could go along on the rescue mission, but she watched enviously as the CARL volunteers, including Doc Tock, rushed out of the room. Then she turned and followed her friends and Colonel Hanson into the examining room.

The puppy was sound asleep on the examining table, snoring softly. His broken leg had been set in a cast. Aside from that he looked happy and peaceful. The Saddle Club watched him sleep for a moment. Then, when a pair of CARL workers came in to move the puppy, the visitors tiptoed out.

When they were back in the reception area, Colonel Hanson glanced at his watch. "Uh-oh, look at the time," he exclaimed. "Your parents are going to think I kidnapped you. It's time to go."

The three girls exchanged glances. They didn't want to leave now—not in the midst of all the excitement. "Can't we stay until they get back with the other animals?" Carole wheedled. "Please?"

"Nope," Colonel Hanson said in a no-nonsense voice.

"It's late, and you have school tomorrow. Besides, you wouldn't want to fall asleep in the middle of that ballet you're seeing, would you? What would the dancers think?"

Reluctantly, the girls followed Colonel Hanson out to the car. As she climbed into the backseat, Lisa started yawning in spite of herself. She had to admit that all the work she'd done taking care of the mare had really worn her out. It would be nice to relax and enjoy *The Nutcracker* the next evening, although she hated the thought that she would have only a few minutes with the mare after school. But after that it would be the weekend, and then it wouldn't be long until Christmas vacation started. Then she would be able to spend all her time with the mare.

She smiled at the thought and settled back against the seat, closing her eyes as the car headed for home.

LISA WAS WHISTLING one of the songs from *The Nutcracker* when she arrived at Pine Hollow the next afternoon. She was looking forward to the ballet. Besides that, for the first time in days she was actually feeling optimistic about things. She had called CARL that morning and found out that the puppy was fine, and that the other animals the rescuers had picked up were also in relatively good shape. None of them was nearly as bad off as the mare had been—aside from some malnutrition and a rash around the goat's neck from being tied up with a dirty rope, there wasn't much wrong with them. The CARL people thought the man probably hadn't had the other animals as long as he'd had the mare.

Now, with the owner of the farm on his way to jail, it

somehow seemed more possible that the mare might recover to take part in a Starlight Ride—not this year, but someday.

But when Lisa turned down the aisle toward the mare's stall, she stopped whistling abruptly. Judy Barker's black bag was sitting in the middle of the aisle in front of the mare's stall, and pieces of equipment were spread all around it. Max and Red were both outside the stall, looking in.

Lisa hurried up to them, her heart in her throat. "What's going on?"

Max turned to her, his face reassuring. "Don't worry, Lisa. She had a rough night and took a turn for the worse. But Judy thinks it's passed now. She's just giving her some shots to make sure."

Lisa gasped. Just when she thought things were getting better, they were really getting worse. She knew there was no way she could enjoy herself at the ballet now. She had to find Carole and Stevie and tell them.

"Excuse me," she said to Max and Red. "I'll be right back." She raced away toward Belle's stall.

Stevie and Carole were both there. As soon as they saw their friend's face, they knew something was wrong.

"It's the mare," Lisa said before they could ask. "Judy's with her now." She told them what Max had told her.

"That's awful," Carole said. "After she seemed to recognize us yesterday, I was hoping she was finally starting to recover."

"Me too," Lisa said. "But now that this has happened, I—I don't think I can go to the ballet tonight. I have to stay here with her. I don't know if it will make any difference, but I have to try. I'm sorry."

"Don't apologize," Stevie said. "We understand."

Carole nodded. "I wish we could all stay," she said. "But we'll be with you in spirit."

"Saddle Club spirit," Stevie added, reaching out to hug Lisa.

Lisa just nodded and hugged her back, not sure she trusted her voice at the moment. It was wonderful to have such understanding friends. "I'll pay your parents back for the ticket," she said when she could speak again. "I promise."

"You probably won't have to," Stevie said. "This performance has been sold out for weeks, and I'll bet people are still trying to get tickets. I'm sure we can sell your seat back to the box office."

Carole squeezed Lisa's arm comfortingly. "I've got to go take care of Starlight now," she said. "We'll come say good-bye before we leave, just in case you change your mind about coming."

"I won't," Lisa said. "But thanks." She hurried back toward the mare's stall as Carole headed for the tack room and Stevie stayed with Belle.

Judy was just emerging from the stall when Lisa got there. "Oh, hello, Lisa," the vet said.

"How is she?" Lisa asked, not even bothering to return Judy's greeting.

"Well, we had a few rough moments there, but I think she's over it now," Judy said, glancing at Max and Red. "We'll want to keep a close eye on her for the next day or so, though."

"That's what I'm here for," Lisa said. "Just tell me what to do."

Judy nodded. "You've been doing a terrific job so far, Lisa," she said. She smiled at Max and Red. "You, too, of course. Mostly you all just need to keep doing more of the same. I'm going to leave a little medicine to mix with her evening feed, and I'll give her another shot in the morning. Other than that, you should just keep a close eye on her and call me if anything looks strange."

"Okay," Lisa said. "Is that all?"

"That's all," Judy said. "Oh, except to keep her company, of course. Let her know you're pulling for her." She winked at Lisa. "That's not exactly the scientific method, but I've seen it work."

Lisa nodded. She was glad to see that Judy was smiling. Maybe that meant the mare wasn't in such bad shape after all. Still, Lisa wasn't taking any chances. She was going to spend every minute she could with the mare. "I'd better go call my parents and tell them I'll be here until late tonight," she said. "I'll be right back."

* * *

109

WHEN CAROLE AND Stevie stopped by the stall half an hour later, Lisa was carefully applying ointment to the worst of the mare's wounds.

"How is she?" Carole asked.

Lisa put the cap back on the ointment and leaned on the stall door to talk to them. "Judy thinks the worst is over."

"Are you sure you don't want to change your mind and come with us?" Stevie asked.

"I'm sure," Lisa replied. "I've got to stay here and keep an eye on her. Judy said the next day or so is critical."

Stevie and Carole nodded, understanding. They said good-bye to Lisa and the mare and then left.

They arrived at Stevie's house a few minutes later and explained the situation to Mr. and Mrs. Lake.

"Oh, that's too bad," Mrs. Lake said when she heard that Lisa wouldn't be coming. "I know how much Lisa loves the ballet. But I'm sure we can get a refund on her ticket."

"Unless there's anyone else you girls can think of who might be able to make it at the last minute," Mr. Lake added. "What about Phil?"

Stevie shook her head. "He's out of town visiting relatives."

"Carole? What about your father? Think he'd be up for it?" Mr. Lake asked.

"I don't think so," Carole said. "He mentioned that he had a lot of paperwork to catch up on tonight. Besides, he's not exactly a big ballet fan."

Mr. Lake laughed. "Got it. Well, we don't have to leave for an hour or so. If you think of anybody else let us know. We'll be ready to eat in a few minutes. Why don't you girls get changed?"

"Okay, Dad," Stevie said. She led the way up to her bedroom. Carole had brought a change of clothes, and soon both girls were dressed and ready. They arrived back downstairs just in time to sit down to a quick dinner.

"You both look lovely," Mrs. Lake said, passing Carole a bowl of rice.

"Thanks," Stevie said. She noticed that Alex was still wearing the jeans he'd worn to school that day. "Hey, is that what you're wearing to the dance?"

"I'm not going," Alex replied.

"What do you mean?" Stevie said. "Just because you're not going with what's-her-name doesn't mean you shouldn't go at all. A lot of kids go stag."

Alex shrugged. "What would be the point?" He stirred the food on his plate aimlessly, without eating any of it.

"He's been like this all day," Chad told Stevie, sounding worried. "I told him he should go and have a good time. That would show her. But he won't listen."

Stevie couldn't really blame Alex for not wanting to go to the dance. She wouldn't, either, in his shoes. That thought made her stop and think. What would she be feeling if she were the one with the broken heart? Even though she certainly wouldn't have been as annoying and sappy as Alex had been, she was sure she'd be just as upset right now. For the first time she started to feel a little guilty about teasing him over the past two days. Before that, when he was still dating Paige, the teasing had been fun. But after they broke up, Stevie realized, it had been more than a little mean.

She gulped. She pretended to hate her brothers, but the truth was she cared about them a lot. She didn't like the thought of Alex sitting home tonight, alone and sad, while she was out having fun.

Before she realized what she was about to say, Stevie spoke up. "Hey, Alex," she said, trying to sound casual. "If you're not going to the dance, why don't you come to *The Nutcracker* with us tonight? Lisa can't go, so we have an extra ticket."

Mrs. Lake's fork stopped halfway to her mouth. Mr. Lake froze in midchew. Chad lifted an eyebrow. Michael almost choked on his milk. And Carole just stared at Stevie in amazement.

Alex took his time answering, and Stevie was sure he was going to say no. She knew that normally he would rather walk barefoot on nails than go to the ballet.

But Alex surprised her. "Sure," he said, trying to sound casual but not quite succeeding. "I guess that would be cool." He took a few quick bites of his food and then stood up. "I'd better go change clothes, right? They probably don't like it if you wear jeans."

Nobody spoke until he had left the room. Then Mr. Lake

turned to Stevie. "I know I told you to think of somebody to invite, but I have to admit I'm surprised," he said. "And pleased."

Stevie shrugged. "No big deal, Dad," she said, picking up her fork. "We had a free ticket, Alex had some free time—it was the perfect solution. I'm just glad he said yes." And to her own surprise, she realized that was absolutely true.

THE STABLE HAD quieted down quickly after Stevie and Carole had left. There weren't many riders around, and those who were there were hurrying to get home for dinner. Soon Lisa was alone with her thoughts and the sounds of horses moving around in their stalls, waiting for their evening meal. She finished dressing the mare's scratches and cuts. They looked as if they were starting to heal. Then she went to find Red.

He was in the grain shed. "Hi, Lisa," he said. "Let me guess. Is that gray mare of yours ready for her dinner?"

Lisa nodded. "I just wanted to remind you to add her medicine to her grain."

Red held up a bucket partly filled with grain. "It's already done. Feel like playing waitress?"

"Sure." Lisa took the bucket and returned to the mare's stall. After she fed her, Lisa left her alone to eat and went to help Red feed the other horses.

When she returned, the mare had stopped eating. Lisa saw that she had finished most of the grain ration and had nibbled at her hay. "You didn't quite clean your plate, but I guess you did pretty well," Lisa said.

She stood outside the stall for a moment watching the mare. By now all the other riders had left, and the other horses were quiet as they munched their dinners. Pine Hollow was as quiet as Lisa had ever heard it. It was a little spooky—as if the whole stable were waiting for something.

To take her mind off those kinds of thoughts, Lisa decided to give the mare a good grooming. She hadn't been outside that day and her coat was pretty clean, but Lisa knew that regular and thorough grooming was one way to get a horse accustomed to being handled.

"Hi there, big girl," Lisa said as she put the mare in crossties and set the grooming bucket where she could reach it. "Ready to have those feet checked out?" Lisa lifted the mare's left front foot. As she did, she continued to talk to her.

"My friends are probably getting ready to leave for the ballet about now," she said. For a moment she felt a little wistful. It would have been fun to be going with them. But that feeling didn't last long. Lisa had an important job to do, and she didn't really regret missing the ballet. She could see

The Nutcracker again another year. "I'd much rather stay here tonight and take extra good care of you," she told the mare, checking the thrush dressing in the foot. She took her time doing it, holding the mare's foot for longer than was strictly necessary. That was partly because she wanted the horse to get used to being fussed over and partly because once it was over she wasn't sure what she was going to do next. "You're getting used to having me take care of you, aren't you?"

The mare didn't respond. Lisa wondered if she even heard her talking. She shrugged. Even if the sound of Lisa's voice in the silence didn't make the horse feel better, it made Lisa feel better. She decided to describe the plot of *The Nutcracker* to the horse, then she proceeded to do so, taking time out from the story to describe the way the costumes usually looked and to explain some basic ballet moves, as well as to hum a couple of the most famous melodies.

"Anyway, *The Nutcracker* is really great, but I've seen it lots of times before," Lisa said at last. By this time she had finished checking three of the mare's feet and was carefully examining the last, most seriously infected one. "I'd much rather be here with you. Because if you get better, that would be the best Christmas present ever. I know you can do it. I just wonder if *you* know it."

She sighed and looked up at the mare's face. To her surprise, the mare was looking back. Lisa let the foot she was working on drop and stood up.

116

"Hey, don't tell me you're actually listening to me?" Lisa said.

The mare let out a small snort and turned her head away. But Lisa could tell by the almost imperceptible twitches of the horse's ears that she wasn't completely disinterested in her presence.

"Well, how about that," Lisa whispered. "You do know I'm here after all." Not wanting to lose the horse's attention now that she finally had it, Lisa continued to talk. She started with the Starlight Ride.

"It's so wonderful," she said, reaching into the grooming bucket and picking up a rub rag. "I'm sure you would love it just as much as everyone else does. Sometimes I think the horses must look forward to it just as much as the people." She began rubbing down the mare's body, beginning behind her ears and working toward her tail.

"It would be really great if you could be in it this year, but I don't think there's any way that will happen," Lisa said. "But maybe if you get better you can be in it next Christmas. If you stay here at Pine Hollow, that is." That was a thought that hadn't occurred to Lisa. What would happen to the mare when she got better? Lisa was pretty sure she would never be returned to her owner. But that didn't necessarily mean she would be allowed to stay on here.

Lisa decided to put the question out of her mind for now. There would be plenty of time to worry about that after the mare was better.

"Anyway, I hope you get to stay here with us. I know you'd like it a lot better than where you used to live," Lisa said. "You've got to believe me when I tell you you've got a long life ahead of you. It could be a happy one if you just give yourself a chance."

She moved around the mare's forequarters and began to rub her other side. Out of the corner of her eye, she thought she saw the horse's head following her movement. But she was afraid to look up and see.

"Sal didn't have that chance, but you do," she continued. "He wasn't as lucky as you were. CARL didn't find him in time to save him. But we're trying to save you. We just need your help." Lisa sighed. "It's always so sad when a horse's life is over. I was very sad when my favorite horse, Pepper, died a while ago." Pepper had helped Lisa learn to love horses and riding. He had been very special to her, but he had eventually become too old and sick to go on. It had been very hard for Lisa to let him go when Max had finally decided to have him put down.

She was silent for a moment, rubbing the mare's hindquarters slowly as she thought about Pepper. He had been a wonderful horse. Then she brought her mind back to the mare. She could be a wonderful horse, too. Lisa was sure of it. She just had to convince the horse of it.

"Anyway, it was sad when Pepper died," Lisa went on. "But at least he'd had a long and happy and satisfying life. It was much sadder when Sal died. He never had the chance

for that kind of life, just because a human was cruel to him."
Her eyes started to fill with tears at the thought, but she
blinked them away. "I don't want the same thing to happen
to you."

She dropped the rub rag in the bucket and looked up, half
afraid that the horse would be standing dejectedly once
again. But she was looking at Lisa. One ear still drooped
lazily, but the other was perked forward.

"You really are listening, aren't you?" Lisa said in wonder.
Somehow, in the silence of the barn, the mare was coming
back to life.

Lisa bent over and picked up the plastic dandy brush. "I
think we can use this today, don't you?" Tentatively, she
held the brush out for the horse's inspection. At first she
thought the mare was going to ignore it. But suddenly her
other ear perked forward and she reached out toward Lisa's
hand. Before Lisa knew what was happening, the horse had
picked up the brush by its plastic handle and was holding it
between her big teeth, looking very pleased with herself.

Lisa couldn't help herself. She burst out laughing. The
mare looked surprised but not frightened at the girl's sudden
outburst.

"What do you think you're doing?" Lisa exclaimed, reaching out for the dandy brush. The mare dodged slightly, moving her head just enough to keep the brush out of Lisa's
reach.

Suddenly Lisa knew what the horse was doing. She was

playing. And if she was playing, that was the most hopeful sign yet. Creatures that had lost the will to live didn't spend their time playing games. Only creatures that wanted to get better did.

Lisa finally got the brush back. "You funny thing," she said, staring at the brush in her hands. "I wonder if you have a taste for plastic. Or maybe you just thought I was being too slow about the grooming."

The horse had quieted down again, but she was still watching Lisa. Lisa reached out to stroke her soft muzzle, and the mare didn't pull away.

"You really are a beauty, do you know that, girl?" Lisa said. And suddenly, calling the mare "girl" didn't seem good enough. "You know what? I think it's time to give you a name," Lisa commented. "In fact, it's past time."

As soon as Lisa started thinking about it, she realized it was easier said than done. She wished Stevie and Carole could be there to help her think of something. But now that she had decided the mare needed a name, Lisa couldn't bear the thought of waiting one minute longer to give her one.

She stared at the mare's pale gray coat. "Well, my first idea is to call you something like Moonlight or maybe Starshine," she told her. "After all, in the right light you glow just like a silvery moon or a bright evening star. But both those names sound too much like Starlight's name. You need your very own name that just sounds like you." Lisa realized her last sentence didn't make much sense, but the mare seemed to understand.

Lisa started to work on the mare's coat with the dandy brush while she thought. "Maybe I should name you after something in *The Nutcracker*, since that's what I'd be seeing right now if not for you," she mused. "What do you think of being called Sugarplum? You know, after the scene with the Dance of the Sugarplum Fairy." Somehow that name didn't seem quite right, either.

Lisa kept thinking. "Well, it is almost Christmas," she said. "You could have a Christmassy name. How about Merry? Or Jingle Bell? Or Holly?" But none of those names seemed to suit the mare, either.

Lisa sighed in frustration and replaced the dandy brush in the bucket, being careful to keep it out of the mare's reach. As she stood up again, she noticed that a piece of straw had become entangled in the mare's mane.

"Let me just get that knot out before I finish brushing you," Lisa said. She grabbed the plastic mane comb out of the bucket and reached for the tangle. But before she could get to work on it, the mare had reached over and nimbly plucked the comb out of Lisa's fingers.

"Hey!" Lisa exclaimed. She smiled at the horse. "I guess my first guess was right. You do have a taste for plastic!"

The mare didn't argue. And she didn't resist when Lisa took the comb back. Instead of continuing with the grooming, Lisa leaned back against the wall and looked at the mare for a moment.

"You know, maybe a miracle will happen after all," she said. "Maybe you will be well enough to be in the Starlight Ride this Christmas Eve."

She knew that wouldn't really happen, but the thought had given her an idea.

"I know!" she exclaimed, so suddenly that the mare perked both ears forward and bobbed her head in alarm. "Sorry," Lisa said soothingly. "But I just thought of the perfect name." She reached forward with the grooming comb and tapped the mare lightly on the nose. "I hereby dub thee Eve. For Christmas Eve, you know. It's perfect—Christmassy and special and pretty. And it just *sounds* like you."

The horse snorted, as if in agreement. Lisa laughed again, and before she realized what she was doing, she had reached out and given Eve a big hug. She felt the horse tense slightly at first and then relax. To Lisa, it almost felt as though Eve was hugging her back.

WHEN JUDY BARKER arrived later, Lisa was just finishing her leisurely grooming. "Hi, Judy," she greeted the vet cheerfully.

Judy looked a little surprised at Lisa's mood. "Hello, Lisa. I just finished a call in the neighborhood, so I thought I'd stop by and see how things are going. So how's our girl?"

"You tell me," Lisa said with a smile, stepping back to let Judy look.

The vet looked the mare over carefully. She checked her temperature, then listened to her breathing and her heart with her stethoscope. Finally she put away her tools and looked at Lisa with a smile. "I'm surprised. I was hoping she'd improve after that last rough spot, but I didn't dare to hope she'd perk up this much. You must have the magic touch, Lisa. For the first time, I feel confident in saying that this horse is on the road to recovery."

"Really?" Lisa said. She turned to the horse and gave her another hug. "Did you hear that, Eve? It's official. You're going to get better."

Seeing the surprised look on Judy's face, Lisa quickly explained how she had come up with the name. "Do you like it?" she asked the vet.

Judy smiled and nodded. "I think it suits her perfectly."

After that, Lisa and Judy just stood quietly for a while, watching as Eve took a few sips of water, chewed a mouthful of hay, and then gradually fell asleep. And without either of them saying so, both of them knew they were watching a horse who had finally found a reason to live.

12

"DID YOU TALK to Lisa last night?" Stevie asked. It was Saturday morning, and she had just met Carole outside Pine Hollow. The girls had a meeting of their Pony Club, Horse Wise, a little later that morning, but they had arrived early because they had wanted to have a chance to talk first. It seemed as though they hadn't had a real Saddle Club meeting in ages.

Carole yawned. "Nope. I was so exhausted when I got home that I went straight to bed. Did you talk to her?"

Stevie shook her head. "I wanted to call her, but my parents wouldn't let me. They said it was too late."

"Let's go inside and see if she's here yet." The two girls hurried into the stable. They checked at the mare's stall first, and that was exactly where they found Lisa.

"You haven't been here all night, have you?" Stevie teased. Without waiting for an answer, she added, "So how is she?"

Lisa smiled. "First of all, we don't have to keep calling her 'she' all the time. She has a name now."

Carole and Stevie looked surprised. "She does?" Carole said. "What is it?"

"Her name is Eve," Lisa said. She waited anxiously for her friends' reactions. She really wanted them to like the name she had chosen.

They did. "It's perfect," Stevie declared. "I couldn't have done better myself."

Her friends couldn't help laughing at that. It had taken Stevie a long time to give Belle her name.

"To answer your question," Lisa said, "Eve is doing very well. She's still got a long way to go, but Judy believes she'll definitely make it. And so do I."

"You must have had some night," Carole said, slowly reaching out to give Eve a pat on the nose. The mare looked a little nervous, but she didn't step away.

"I did," Lisa said. "Or should I say, *we* did." She glanced at Eve. "Last night I realized that if I really wanted her to get better, I had to let her know. Otherwise she might not think anybody cared."

"How could she think that?" Stevie asked. "You've been spending practically every second of the day with her since she got here."

125

"I know," Lisa said. "I was being very careful to take perfect care of her medical problems and stuff, and in that way I was caring about her a lot. But in another way, I was also being careful not to let myself get too attached to her. I was afraid of how much that would hurt if she died."

Carole watched the mare, who was chewing on a mouthful of hay, and thought about that for a second. "I guess that makes sense," she said slowly. "I mean, we were all afraid even to give her a name, weren't we?"

Lisa nodded. "We were holding back. I didn't realize it until last night, because I thought I was caring as much as I could. But I finally realized that if I *really* wanted her to get better I had to let myself care all the way. Naming her helped me do that, if you know what I mean."

Her friends did. "Well, I guess you were right," Stevie said. "It worked."

"I know. And I'm glad," Lisa said. "But even if it hadn't, I would still be glad I figured it out."

"I guess that's what my dad calls a life lesson," Carole said.

Lisa smiled. "Hey, by the way, how was the ballet?" she asked, leaning back against the stall door.

"It was great," Carole said.

Stevie agreed. "And guess who ended up using your ticket?" she asked. "Actually, never mind, you'll never guess. It was Alex."

"Alex who?" Lisa asked.

126

"Alex Lake," Stevie said. "My brother. I asked him if he wanted to come with us, and he said yes."

"Wait a minute," Lisa said, holding up one hand. "You asked *him*? What's going on here? Did pigs start flying and I didn't hear about it?"

Carole giggled. "No, it's true. I'm a witness." She quickly told Lisa the whole story.

"Well, I'm glad you finally gave poor Alex a break," Lisa said. She jumped a little as she felt a large nose begin snuffling at the back of her neck.

"Wow! She really knows you now, Lees," Stevie exclaimed with delight.

"She's a whole new horse," Carole added, grinning widely.

"Anyway," Stevie said as the mare went back to her breakfast, "I was super nice to Alex through the whole ballet."

"True," Carole confirmed. "She was a perfect gentlewoman. And I think Alex appreciated it, too. Even if he doesn't usually like ballet, this was just the thing he needed to take his mind off not being at the dance with Paige."

"In more ways than one," Stevie added. "Not only did it take his mind off his broken heart, but it may actually have cured it."

"What do you mean?" Lisa asked.

Carole picked up a spare bucket and turned it upside down to create a makeshift chair. It was early, and she had been up late the night before, and she was tired. "We ended up sitting one row behind a classmate of Alex and Stevie's at the ballet," she said. "A girl named Susie and her parents."

Stevie grinned. "By the end of the evening, my brother had mysteriously cheered up quite a bit. And Susie looked pretty happy, too."

"Oh, no," Lisa said with a groan. "Don't tell me—are we about to witness the return of Alex, the world's greatest romantic?"

"Looks that way," Stevie said, still smiling.

Lisa raised one eyebrow suspiciously. "Why do you look so happy about it? I thought he drove you crazy when he was going out with Paige."

"Sure," Stevie said. "But it also gave me some great teasing opportunities. Let me tell you, it was a real effort to be nice to him for a whole evening. It would be a relief to have something new to give him a hard time about."

Carole and Lisa laughed. The mare watched them curiously.

Stevie looked at Eve with interest. "It's really amazing," she said. "It's like she suddenly remembered she had a personality."

"I know," Lisa said. "She's actually quite playful when she wants to be." She told her friends about Eve's taste for plastic.

"I'd bet anything that horrible man didn't have her for

128

her whole life," Carole said, standing up and fishing a small piece of carrot out of her jeans pocket. She held it out to the mare. Eve sniffed at it for a few seconds, then gently lifted the carrot from Carole's palm. "She must have had another owner before him who treated her well. Otherwise she wouldn't be able to trust people at all."

Lisa gasped. "Oh, I almost forgot to tell you," she said. "I talked to the police again this morning. And you're exactly right."

"What do you mean?" Carole asked, watching the mare crunch the carrot eagerly. "What did they say?"

"Well, first of all they told me that they have officially confiscated all the animals that were on that farm and turned them over to CARL," Lisa said. "That means CARL can go ahead and place them in new homes. A family with a little boy has already asked to adopt the puppy we found. They're just waiting until his foot is better. But he should be with his new family by Christmas."

"Oh, how wonderful!" Stevie said. "What about the other animals?"

"The CARL people think they'll be able to place them, too," Lisa said. "It sounds like the farmer whose barn burned down may take the goat and the chickens when he takes his own animals back. That just leaves the other dog. He seems like a pretty well trained watchdog, so they're sure somebody will want him, too."

"That must have been the watchdog barking when we

first went to the farm," Carole said distractedly. She was busy trying to convince the mare that she didn't have any more carrots by letting her snuffle at her hand.

Lisa nodded. "Anyway, they questioned that nasty man further and found out he'd only had Eve for about six months. Her last owner was a woman who died of cancer. The woman's children didn't have any place to keep a horse, so they sold her cheap to the first person to make an offer."

"I wonder why a horrible man like that would want a horse in the first place?" Stevie commented.

"I don't know," Lisa said with a shudder. "But the important thing is that Eve is away from him now for good."

Carole glanced from Lisa to the mare and back again. There was a question she wanted to ask, but she wasn't quite sure how to phrase it. "Um, so what's going to happen to her now?" she asked. "Once she's all better, that is."

Lisa gulped. "I've been wondering about that, too," she admitted. "The police said the CARL people have decided that if Max is willing, they'd be grateful if she could stay on here at Pine Hollow until they find someone to adopt her."

"I hadn't even thought about that," Stevie said. "But I guess she'll have to leave sooner or later. That's sad, isn't it?"

Lisa nodded. "It's okay," she said, trying to sound as if she meant it. "I'm just glad she's better. That's the only important thing."

"Why don't we take advantage of her while we've got her by giving her a good grooming?" Carole suggested. "We have plenty of time before we have to start getting ready for Horse Wise."

"Sounds good to me," Stevie said. She turned to Lisa. "Do you think she'll get too nervous having all of us work on her?"

"There's only one way to find out," Lisa said. She put the mare in cross-ties and the girls got started. They decided to work in shifts, with one person sitting on the bucket and watching while the other two did the grooming. Eve seemed a little nervous about the arrangement at first, but after Lisa let her chew on the dandy brush for a few minutes, she calmed down.

As she worked, Lisa couldn't help thinking about the mare's future. She had meant what she said about being happy Eve was better. But she knew she'd be even happier if she knew what kind of future lay ahead for Eve. After all, who knew what kind of person might end up adopting her? What if it was someone who didn't appreciate her properly? Or, even worse, someone who wouldn't treat her well? Lisa knew that CARL was very careful to check out the people who adopted their animals, but everyone made mistakes. In any case, Eve was going to need special care for quite a while to make sure she was completely recovered from her ordeal. What if her new owner didn't realize that?

"How's it going, girls?" said a familiar voice, jolting Lisa out of her thoughts.

"Hi, Max," Stevie said, jumping up. It was her turn to watch from the bucket, and she didn't want Max to think she was just sitting around with nothing to do. "We're just, um, grooming the mare."

"So I see," Max said, with a twinkle in his blue eyes that reassured Stevie that she wasn't about to be ordered to start mucking out stalls. The mare had started rolling her eyes when Max appeared, but she didn't try to get away. Max took a few steps back and the mare calmed down. "She's looking much better today."

Lisa nodded, glad that Max had noticed. "It's because she decided she wants to get better," she told him.

Some people might have laughed at a statement like that, but Max Regnery wasn't one of them. "So I see," he said again. He paused, looking the mare over thoughtfully. "Red believes she's getting over her nervousness with men, and I think he may be right. And she certainly seems to have taken to you girls. I think she's going to make someone an awfully fine riding horse when she gets better. Judy thinks she's only seven or eight years old. She's got a long future ahead of her."

"She definitely does," Lisa said, not looking up from the brush she was running over Eve's withers. "I just hope she gets an owner who will really appreciate her. And take good care of her."

"Oh, I'm sure she will," Max said. He watched the girls work in silence for another minute or two.

Finally Lisa couldn't take it anymore. "But what if she doesn't?" she burst out. "She just decided life is worth living again. What if someone awful adopts her and ruins all that?"

Max took his time answering. "I don't think that's going to happen," he said at last. "Actually, I was just coming to tell you the news. I just spoke to the folks at CARL, and the mare has officially been adopted."

Lisa's heart plummeted into her stomach. She knew she was going to have to adjust to Eve's leaving. She just hadn't thought it would happen so soon. "She has?" she said, trying to keep her voice steady.

Max nodded. "She has," he said.

"Is the new owner anybody we know?" Stevie asked, hoping that at least they would still be able to visit the mare.

"Oh, yes," Max said. "It's someone you know very well indeed. In fact, it's me."

Lisa gasped. "You? You mean you're Eve's new owner?" Her heart soared. That meant Eve wouldn't be leaving Pine Hollow. Lisa could still see her almost every day, maybe even ride her when she was better. It meant that Eve would have her chance to take part in the Starlight Ride next Christmas after all.

"Eve?" Max looked confused for a second. Then his face cleared. "Let me guess. You've already named my new mare for me."

133

"Oh. I guess we have," Lisa said. "I was calling her Eve. I thought of it last night. Do you like it?"

"I love it," Max assured her. "She looks just like an Eve to me."

"But Max, what made you decide you needed another horse?" Stevie asked.

Max shrugged. "Part of what convinced me was the mare—er, that is, Eve—herself. She's got good lines under all those cuts and bruises, and she's still young enough to train if she isn't fully trained already. And I've seen enough to make me think she probably is, and will just need a little reminding. The other thing is that I've been thinking it's almost time to let old Nero have a rest. Eve can be his replacement." Nero was the oldest horse at Pine Hollow. He was still a gentle, reliable stable mount, but The Saddle Club knew that in horse years he was older than any of their grandparents.

Hearing about Nero's impending retirement made Lisa think about her one-sided conversation with Eve the night before. It made her a little sad to think that Nero was retiring, just as Pepper had before him, and that his life was drawing to a close. But it also made her happy to think that Eve was going to be there to carry on Nero's duties. It would be almost as if she were carrying on his spirit, as well as the spirits of Pepper and all the other Pine Hollow horses who had come before her. As Lisa was learning in her ecology project, life almost always found a way to go on, through the changing seasons and the passing years. Eve would be a part of life; she wouldn't be doomed to miss it as poor Sal had.

Lisa wasn't sure how to express all of this to Max in words, so she didn't try. She just handed the dandy brush to Eve, who grabbed it, and hurried over to give Max a big hug.

He looked surprised but pleased. He hugged her back for a moment, then gently disentangled himself. "All right, that's enough talking," he said briskly. "Now I want to see you girls getting back to work. And see that you take good care of my new horse." With that, he turned on his heel and marched away.

Carole giggled as she watched him go. "I don't believe it, Lisa," she said. "I think you actually embarrassed him."

Lisa giggled, too. "I know. But isn't it wonderful?"

Carole and Stevie weren't sure if she was talking about embarrassing Max or about Max adopting Eve. They decided it was both.

"It's the best pre-Christmas present anyone could ask for," Stevie answered for both of them. Then the three friends all shared a big, unembarrassed, three-way Saddle Club hug.

ABOUT THE AUTHOR

BONNIE BRYANT is the author of many books for young readers, including novelizations of movie hits such as *Teenage Mutant Ninja Turtles* and *Honey, I Blew Up the Kid*, written under her married name, B. B. Hiller.

Ms. Bryant began writing The Saddle Club in 1986. Although she had done some riding before that, she intensified her studies then and found herself learning right along with her characters Stevie, Carole, and Lisa. She claims that they are all much better riders than she is.

Ms. Bryant was born and raised in New York City. She still lives there, in Greenwich Village, with her two sons.